CHAPTER 1

A good day for it, the old professor thought.
Clutching the book under his arm He just needed to
get this sorted, he had been pondering for a week or
more, on what to do. Should he dismiss this irksome
idea. If he left it unsolved, he would always wonder,
what if.
The professor was quite a well know figure in his
north London suburb.
He gave lectures, and tutoring at the local college,
teaching modern sciences. The local people were
more acquainted with his dress sense. He always
wore a three-piece suit, bow tie, and invariably a
fedora hat. He proceeded along the high street,
eager to get to his destination, now he had made up
his mind at last.
The police station was one of the last stations to
survive through to the modern age, with its warm
red brickwork intact. It had an aura officialdom that
modern office buildings lack. Most now incorporated
in glass and concrete bland buildings.
But this time he paused at the steps
leading up to the old red bricked
Police station.
Would this be a fool's errand he
thought, could I be wasting police

time. The worse thing that could happen, he could be humoured, and politely asked, to be on his way. None the less gritting his teeth, a sharp intake of breath he entered.

"Yes Sir, May I help you, the desk Sergeant asked.

Is it possible to have a word with a Detective?

In connection with what Sir

I'M not sure if a crime has been committed

Do you know what sort of crime?

Well, I'm not sure of that either, that's why I need some advice on the matter.

The desk Sergeant studied the man before him. He looked quite normal, not one of your regular misfits, who come in to report the most ludicrous crimes of the day.
I will enquire if there's any one available, Have a seat in the waiting area. Can I take your name Sir?

Certainly Roberts, Professor George

2

Roberts.

The professor sat on the metal seats
bolted to the floor, little else
here except for crime stoppers
posters on the wall, also a
Kitchener type recruitment poster,
The Police Need You, pointing a
large finger at the reader.
Obviously not aimed at an overweight
seventy-year-old man.

A slim man came from behind the
locked door beside the main desk.

'Hello, are you Professor Roberts

'Yes, I am. The desk Sergeant
informed me you would like to report
a crime.

"Well, I am not sure at this stage.

Come into the office Professor, have
a seat, I'm Detective Constable
Russell
Now, what sort of crime, do you want
to report'

"Well as I said before I am not sure,
if this is a crime, or just an old
man's foolish brain being overactive.

Well Just start at the beginning, to
give me an idea of the crime, that
you think was committed. I will take
it from there.

I purchased a job lot, a box of
mixed bric-a-brac from an auction
house in Finchley.
I came across this book amongst
other items in the box, when I
flipped through it, I noticed
someone had written on a page I'm
also aware that's not unusual, being
a teacher at the college.
But it bothered me, if it was
genuine, A gut feeling if you like.
This is the book Grimm's fairy tales;
I placed a marker on the relevant
page.

Detective Russell read the marked
passage,
Em! This could be just childish
scrawling by someone

HELP ME
IT'S May 20th, 2004
I HAVE BEEN TAKEN
AGAINST MY WILL
MY NAME IS REBECCA FINKLESTEIN
I'M 17yrs OLD
I DON'T WANT TO DIE
I LIVE AT 23 WOOD?

4

I'm aware it could be just that.

Have you inquired about the book at the Auction house Sir?

No, I was unsure about it, but I thought I would report it to you, as it was on my mind since I read it

Detective Russell looked at the professor, then back to the book I will take some details first.
Name sir!

George Roberts, Professor

date of birth

3/6/46

Address sir!

Strawberry Cottage Oarlock Lane Hendon

Do you have a contact number?

You can contact me at Victoria college during office hours or my home address.

Very well, would you Wait here I will have a word with my governor about this, I won't keep you too long.

Professor Roberts sat there
patiently waiting, perhaps they are
in there thinking what a silly old
fool I am.

Excuse me Gov, there is an old
gentleman downstairs, he brought in
this book. He bought from the local
auction house. He found a. message
written inside, when he looked at it,
he thought perhaps it was genuine. A
gut feeling, he said.

"Gut feelings I had plenty of gut
feelings on the horses I bet on
never helped me that's for sure.
What do you make of him then Jim,
not one of the usual riff Raff's, is
he.

Well going by his appearance and
manor. NO. He is a professor at the
college, seems genuine type to me.

Have you noticed the date here Jim,
that is ten years ago, this book
could have been floating around for
years, anyone could have written in
the book, now it's landed up in an
auction? He said he had a gut
feeling

I'LL tell you what Jim, you're at the Court later today. Humour him, take a statement from him, then you can go over to the library, after the court. See what they say about the book. Then go and see this Rebecca Finklestein, tell her you're from the library police, tell her not to deface public books. You alright with that Jim.

Yes Vince, fine by me.

With that the detective returned with a slight grin on his face,

Ah, Right Sir! My boss will investigate this, if you make a formal statement, we will get this looked at, we also need to keep the book. If you have any receipts etc., can you leave them at the front desk addressed to me Detective Russell

"Thanks for your time, Detective, should I call back.

No that won't be necessary Sir I will contact you once we have made some enquiries.

CHAPTER 2

The library building in Finchley seemed to be the hub of the local community, posters everywhere advertising all sorts, from Yoga to car boot sales, gardening clubs etc. I was directed to the Head librarian's office

Excuse me Mrs Alexander, a Detective Russell wishes to speak with you.

Come in detective, how may I help you.

We are looking for some information on a book taken out from here in 2004
2004 that's some time ago, not sure all the old type of files was transferred onto our computer systems.
Do you have any details of the book, the name of the book?

Yes, it's Grimm's fairy tales, it was taken out last on 16th May 2004 it has a reference number, FL/08941980/Fl43
Would you be able to tell who the lender was?

If we still have the record yes, I'll go and check, see what I can

8

find in the records.
I would say this maybe a long shot,
but I will see what I can come up
with,
Would you like a tea or coffee
whilst your waiting?

That would be nice, tea milk two
sugars please.
I will send someone in with it.

Detective Russell had long since
finished his tea, now getting a bit
impatient, as time ticked by

"Sorry to have kept you so long
Detective.
It seems the records indicate a,
Miss R. Finklestein, was the last
person to loan the book, which she
never returned.

That is good news Mrs Alexander,
you've been very helpful. are you
sure it was miss Rebecca Finklestein?

Yes

Did you know her by any chance?

No, I'm new to the area

Is this address far from here do you
know?

9

Not sure, there's a local street map
that should help you by the front
lobby entrance on the wall Anything
else I can help you with.

No, you've been more than helpful.

Finding the street map by the
entrance was a lot quicker than
waiting for Mrs Alexander.
Red dot indicates library, now let's
see 24 Woodside Grange Road, not too
far. About ten minutes away, I would
guess.
Parking across the road he could
take in the full scope of the
1920/1930 house, large yes, a family
home, so Miss Finklestein let's see
what you have to say for yourself,
no bell just a large brass type
knocker, giving it a large rap. The
noise that it made, could wake the
dead, I could hear some movement
from inside.

Yes, boomed the man in gym wear with
earphones in, as the door opened.

I'm Detective Russell, as he showed
his Warrant card,
I am trying to find the whereabouts
of Rebecca Finklestein, I was given
this as her home address.

"No, I cannot help you there, we have only been here a couple of years, it was empty when we purchased it a couple of years ago, the neighbours they have been here longer than us, old folks they may be of more help.

Sorry to have troubled you sir

That's OK, sorry I could not help you more Detective

The house to the right, same large type of property a bit run down if anything, at least it has a doorbell and a name Mr & Mrs Tafler.
Not a sound from inside, on a closer look, the net curtains looked a bit drab and forgotten,
I hear the lock being turned; ah someone is in he thought
An old Jewish lady peaked her head around the door, who are you, what do you want.
Sorry to trouble you, I'm Detective Constable Russell, I was at the house next door they said you may be able to help me with my enquiries, as you have lived here for quite some time.
I was looking for the whereabouts of a Rebecca Finklestein who

11

Disappeared in 2004. I understand
she lived next door at that time.
Would you have remembered her at
all'?

Why do you want to know she muttered,
as she lifted herself up to a more
upright position, "that's a long
time ago?

Just some routine questions we wish
to clear up, she's not in any
trouble, just need to have a word
with her.
I know she stayed there, but not for
long, pretty girl, lovely long black
hair.
Is she living locally do you know,
or any of the family?
He asked
She wasn't family just visiting

Not Finklestein family you say,

No, it was the Kaufman family, Jack
Kaufman, his wife and children who
lived there.
I believe she was American or
Canadian, not too sure

Any Kaufman, live here about, do you
know

Not to my knowledge, they also moved

12

away after the girl disappeared.
Something was not right a lot of
coming and going with people, and
the police.
I thought you would know that being
a policeman.

Before my time.

Anything else you can tell me Mrs
Tafler that you can remember.

The house was empty for a long, long
time, squatters moved in for a while
until the new folk moved in a couple
of years ago.

I will leave you my card, if you
remember anything more, please give
me a call, do you know who lives on
the other side of the house.

That will be William Tomb,
He moved here about the same time as
we did.

Well thanks again for your help.

Mr Tombs house seemed to be in a bit
of neglect as was Mrs Tafler house,
must be old money as they say, given
their age's
Ringing the doorbell did not get any
response either, but again he tried

13

once more, this time the door opened
a tall, elegant man stood there, in
his early seventies well dressed.

May I help you he enquired,

Yes, I'm Detective Constable Russell,
showing his identity card to the
gentleman, who took the warrant card
in his hand studying Russell at the
same time

 Are you Mr Tomb

"Yes Detective, how may I help you

I'm making enquiries to the
whereabouts of a Miss R Finklestein
who disappeared in 2004 who I
believe lived next door to you, at
that time

Yes, the American girl, pretty,
shame about her really.

"In what way Sir.

"Well, she disappeared, you should
know that

"So, I'm led to believe Sir

Would you mind if I came in Mr Tomb,

14

perhaps you can give me some more
details?

Yes, come in,

The flooring in the hall was covered
in neatly laid out newspapers, as
was the other rooms, he led him
through to the kitchen.

Excuse me Detective I was having
something to eat, if you don't mind,
take a seat.

As I was saying I'm trying to
establish the whereabouts of Miss R
Finklestein, I believe she lived
next door in 2004, she is not in any
trouble, I just need to talk to her,
to help in our enquiries.

I would presume a lot of people
Would like to talk to her. As I said
earlier, she Disappeared

Disappeared Mr Tomb

Yes, apparently, she never returned
home after going out one morning,
everyone was so upset
The police searched everywhere.
They even searched my garden, al
through my house, even my
Observatory at the top of the house,

15

I'm a bit of a night Owl Star Gazing.
All the other neighbours went
through the same.
Are you not aware of this Detective?
surely you would know all about this.

Before my time Sir!

Well sometime after she disappeared
the Kaufman. family also moved away,
it stood empty for years, fine house
like that

Do you know where they moved to.

"No, But I believe I did Hear they
went towards Essex area.

If I need to, I may call again, Mr
Tomb, I will leave you my card in
case you remember anything else.

Detective Russell sat in his car
looking at the House, thinking that,
perhaps that book that the professor
brought in may have some importance
after all.
Detective Russell reported back to
his superior detective Vincent Lusty
 I believe Sir, this was a police
case back in the 2004 The neighbours
were surprised I was making
enquiries now, as it was so long-ago
statements were made at the time.

16

Leave it with me I will make some
enquiries to see what's what.
Meanwhile go down to the auction
house in the morning, find out who
put this stuff in, to be sold. I may
have some more information by then
on this old case.

Yes Sir!

CHAPTER 3

Finchley was always busy with
traffic, sometimes you could walk
faster than the traffic crept along,
fortunately the auction house
Fraser's was off the main
thoroughfare, they had a small
loading bay area which was helpful
for parking.

You cannot park here this is a
loading bay, the young lad shouted

I won't be long, is your boss here I
enquired.

Mr Fraser is in his office upstairs
mate, You the Police!

Do have you a problem with that

Na, just knew didn't I

Can you point me in the right
direction?

I will take you up, be careful of
this stuff, it's worth a lot of
money some of it.

Old brown furniture with boxes piled
high with assorted bric-a-brac,
painting, and pictures, all piled
against walls.
My escort, pointed to a set of
stairs at the end of the corridor.

Mr Fraser office up there he barked
at me

Thanks.

The office door was open

Mr Fraser, I enquired,

Yes, as he looked up from his
newspaper
What can I do for you

I'm Detective Russell, as he showed
his Warrant card,
Come in take a seat, what can I do
for you.

We are trying to trace an item sold
at one of your auctions some time
ago.
Do you have a date?

About four weeks ago, the purchaser
was a Professor Roberts.

Yes, we know the old professor.

Do you know what sort of items

A small book stand, and a job lot,
box of bric-a-brac
do you have an address?

Roberts yes, Strawberry cottage
Oarlock Lane Hendon.
let's have a look in the ledger
first, four weeks you say, ah yes
Roberts. Yes, book shelve, also two
boxes of junk, ah I mean bric-a-brac.

That would be on our Friday sale
21/06/2014

Do you know who put the box of bric-
a-brac into the sale.

Not unless they had already boxed it
up themselves, often people just
come in with carrier bags full old
odds and ends, we box them up,
easier to sell that way, people can

19

have a shifty through them as such.
Looking at the list there is a Mr
Khan, who entered a single bed,
bookcase, two boxes of mixed items,
they maybe what you're looking for.

Can I take the details of Mr Khan?

Certainly! No point in asking what
this is about?

I'm afraid not, but you have been
most helpful, Mr Fraser
Address is 117 Union Street.
Finchley, contact phone, and mobile
number in case we needed to contact
him.
Thanks once again Mr Fraser.
Time to return to the office, see if
the boss has come up with, any other
leads.
No sooner had I got into the station,

"Jimmy the boss wants you in his
office A S P shouted Val Oats

OK, I could see the boss had company,
were busy chatting away, sharing
some details by the look of it.

Come in Russell, this is Chief
inspector Tony Knight, and inspector
Bob Grant from the Yard, this is one

20

of our detectives Jimmy Russell,
both men had firm handshakes as I
sat down. Knight had an air about
him, being tall and fair, one of the
old school Detectives, been there
done that, Grant was a lot heavier,
but not as tall as Knight, he seemed
a little edgy.

I will bring you up to speed Russell,
these gentlemen were working on a
case back in 2004 a young girl
Rebecca Finklestein, disappeared
it's an unsolved crime, at present,
but it seems that book, with the
name R Finklestein, is the name of
the girl that disappeared, back then.

We have brought some files over with
us, said Bob Grant, not a lot in
here, but it confirms, this seems to
be the same girl. It became an
international case, as the girl in
question was a visiting American.
But the case went cold, next to no
leads.

Bobs going to join you on this Jimmy.

Perhaps we can get it wrapped up
said Tony Knight

How did you get on at the Auction
house Jim?

21

Well, I've traced the person who put the stuff in Vince, I have his details, a Mr Khan he stays in Finchley, next move is to have a word with him.
Vince, has agreed that you pair up for this, see where it goes if it develops, we will get some help in. You two get going, I will talk to you later.

Fancy a quick pint Jim, Bob suggested I can put you in the picture on what we have.

Sounds good to me.

The Three Bells was the regular jaunt, for most of the station.

Here we go, what's your poison Bob

Bitter's fine, I'll get a seat.

Good health Jim.

Well, the girl disappeared on Tuesday 19/05/2004 no one seemed to know why. Apparently, she was a quiet girl. She done a lot of studying in her room.
It seems what they knew of her. Was what she wanted them to know,

nothing came voluntary from her.
They only came to this assumption,
after she disappeared, and all the
questions were asked about her, they
realised that they knew very little,
about their house guest.
When her room was searched, just
some clothes, hardly any paperwork
they found her Passport, but that
turned out to be counterfeit.
The Lewinsohn girl who was about the
same age as her. She thought she was,
pre-occupied, with something,
sometimes a bit distant No girly
talk, never seemed really relaxed.

The Americans were all over the case
for a while, tried to track her
movements here, and in America, drew
a blank. The only thing they managed
to find out, there was a black boy
seen with her at one time. She had
come home with a bruised eye; her
excuse was she knocked herself
accidentally. At the time we believe
he could have something to do with
her disappearance. Even with a wide
Newspaper appeal. It seemed every
road we went down was a dead end. We
were clutching at straws for some
progress, with the boy.
So, Jim, this could be a small
window of opportunity to put the
pieces together. Knowing she was at

the library that day. This book
thing. Is more than we had
discovered. She was never positively
placed anywhere, rightly or wrongly,
no one said they saw a girl matching
her description, absolutely no one
had come forward.

Let's go and see this Mr Khan.

CHAPTER 4

A typical semi, some building work
going on, a nice car on the drive
As we approached the door it was
opened by a young Asian man 35/45.
"Can I help you, he ventured

Hello Sir, I'm Detective Russell and
this is Detective Grant
Would you be MR A Khan.

Yes,

"May we come in and have word Mr
Khan, nothing to worry about, you're
not in trouble.
Shall we go inside sir, it's just
some details you may be able to
assist us with, on an ongoing
enquiry. As I said, you've done

nothing wrong. It's your address,
that brought us here.
When did you move in here Mr Khan?

April 2006, do you own the house or
rent

No, we bought it through Jacobson's

We believe you put some items into
Fraser's Auction house in 21/06/14

Oh yes, I cleared out the garage, we
are turning it into another bedroom.

Were the items you put into the
Auction your property.

Some were, some went to the tip
other things to the Charity shop.

Were they brought here, when you
moved in.

No, no they were here when we moved
in, they were in the house I cleared
the rooms out, just put the stuff in
the garage, been in there for years
out of the way. We started doing
this work, I needed to clear the
garage out.
That's why we sorted stuff for the
Auction, Charity shop, the rest was
pretty much our rubbish due to the

work going on, that went to the dump

These Auction items, A single bed.
Bookshelf, bedside cabinet some
clothes a lamp also books

Yes, that's about it

The clothes, coat jumper etc. shoes,
they were in good condition, so my
wife put them to the charity shop.

Which shop was that Sir?

Heart foundation I believe, I can
check with my wife.

Can you give us a description at all?

They seemed good quality, my wife
thought so, that's why she donated
them

Can we get back to the books Sir,
were they yours, or were they with
the items left here.

No, they were on the small bookshelf,
a couple in the bedside cabinet,
also some handcuffs in the drawer I
just chucked them into a cardboard
box with the small table lamp.

Handcuffs, like toy ones

26

No, a real set, they were in the
bedside cabinet drawer

Were they in the box you put to the
Auction

No, my little boy found them, he
wanted them to play with

Do you still have them?

If we have them, they would be in
our son's room
Russell, and Grant, looked at one
another in surprise when Mr Khan
went off to find them
Are you thinking what I'm thinking
Jim
It's getting interesting, that's for
sure.

There you go gentleman, one set of
handcuffs.

These were with all the other things
you say.

"Yes.

You're sure, they were here when you
moved in, in the same room

Yes, most of the stuff was in one

room.

May we have a look at the room Sir

Can you tell me what's going on here,
I've been very helpful, but how does
all this have to do with me?

Unfortunately, Mr Khan, at this
stage we are not at liberty to
disclose any details, but it looks
like your property may have a
connection with a cold case we are
re-examining.
You have been very helpful, but we
believe our inquiries date before
your occupancy.
It would be helpful if we could have
a little look round the house
especially the room where this stuff
was left.

OK, the room is upstairs, I'll take
you up. It was this room all that
stuff came from.

Could you leave us, Mr Khan, we will
see you downstairs shortly?

"Of course

The room was about 14×14, window
overlooks the back garden, typical
back bedroom for these sizes of

houses, hallway, bathroom a further
boxroom and another double
overlooking the front of the house.
Downstairs hallway, lounge at the
front, dining room at the rear,
French doors to the garden and small
kitchen again door to rear garden.

Thank you, Mr Khan, we may have to
return, there may be some other
questions, that may arise.
Can you give me some contact details?

Yes house & mobile OK

That will do nicely.

Mr Russell this is my wife, Ali.

Pleased to meet you.
Your husband was telling us you put
some clothes to the charity shop.

Yes, the heart shop on the parade

Can you remember anything about the
clothes at all?

Well, they did seem quite newish, if
I remember right, that's why we put
them to the charity shop

Anything else, Female, Male, colour.

Oh female, jeans, jumper female type
not sure of colour, a red fleece
type of coat, trainers, Oh, a bra.

That's ideal, gives us an idea about
things, did you notice a size   for
any of the clothes, by any chance
12/14 I think, too big for me.

Well thank you both again Mr & Mrs
Khan, we may return at some stage,
we will be in contact.

I think we better go and see the
boss; this looks promising Bob; He
might have some more info on things.
Yes, on the original inquiry there
was Simply no leads to go on, it was
very frustrating, this seems a
better start this time.

CHAPTER 5

The squad room was buzzing a work
board was up some details of Rebecca
Finklestein, her photo blown up from
her passport.

What's the story from Mr Khan Bob.

The auction items were in the house when he moved in, that would be 2006 He could not tell us a lot, but amongst the items were these handcuffs

These were there when he moved in.

Hand cuffs said Vince, in amazement.

Yes apparently, I double checked.

How come he still had them.

There little boy found them in the bedside cabinet when they were clearing out the stuff, he wanted to play with them.

Right, everyone, listen up we need to fill in all the missing blanks to this enquiry.
Someone checks, the land registry, see who owned this house before the Khans, a couple of you go down to the Road, get on the knockers around the neighbours, see if anybody remembers seeing a girl at the address, someone must have seen her, check the electoral roll that may give us some info.
I can access that on the computer Gov, shouted Danny Addis our computer geek.

31

OK get to it boys let's get this
rolling before the yanks come
barging in again.
Addis found no one on the electoral
roll, other than Mr Khan. But
checking land registry came up with
the previous owner Mr Abel Yudin,
that tied up with the selling agents.
Let's go and see them, see what they
know of Mr Yudin and his little
house.

Jacobson's was an old established
agent, dealing with the Jewish
community overall.

Good morning, who's in charge please,
Bob asked the front of office
receptionist.

Mr Jacobson.

We would like to see him, is he
available.

The receptionist looked at her desk
monitor, he has a client now, he
will be finished shortly, would you
care to have a seat.

Yes fine. Jim was looking at the
prices of the housing stock as they
sat there, need to earn a good wage
to afford one of these Bob.

Yes, even to rent somewhere is expensive this part of London.

A couple appeared from the rear hallway, with that the receptionist asked the waiting detectives their names and business, Jim replied to Detective Russell and Detective Grant police business.
The receptionist relayed their details over the phone, then a gentleman came through the rear hallway, his hand out to shake Their hands.

Good morning gentlemen come through.

He led us into his office at the rear of the hallway.

Take a seat, how may I help you.

We are conducting some enquiries, regarding a property you sold in Union Street number 117. the purchaser's name is Khan

I'll look at the records, yes, a Mr Khan purchased the property in 2006

Who was the seller.

That would be Abel Yudin, Gentlemen.

33

Do you have contact details for Mr Yudin, Mr Jacobson?

Yes, everyone knows Mr Abel Yudin.

He stays just off the North circular road Chambers Road, a very desirable area to live

What number would that be.

House name, no number RAGMEN

Ragmen funny name for a house

Not really, his father was a tailor it was his house before Abel moved in.

Is Abel Yudin also a tailor then, how would you describe Mr Yudin

No, He is a meat wholesaler, provides all the local butchers and stores with their Kosher meat requirements, Short stocky very forward but helpful, he does not suffer fools gladly, married two children.

Has he owned that property long.

Yes, it was in a portfolio of his fathers. Old man Yudin had a little letting business on the side, apart from his tailoring shop, he had quite a few at one time, but Abel sold some off, too busy in his own business to look after them. I don't think he is a good landlord like his father was.

Do you know anything about Mr Khan the purchaser?

Only that he could afford the house, even offered well over the asking price as I recall, they had relatives living close by, may have been a factor.

Thanks for your help, Mr Jacobson

"No problem.

"Right, Chambers Road then Bob.

Mr Jacobson was right, these houses were in a different league altogether, larger properties, many with high iron gates and fences, this looks like the one Jim. Yes, RAGMEN cut into a large rock by the gate double fronted house, nice front lawn curved driveway in, very nice. they drove up to the front of the property, three cars, nice little sports job as well.

35

Big Ben chimes from the doorbell, a spacious hallway they could see through the glass panel door, they could hear someone shouting inside. "Someone at the front door" a woman appeared at the far end of the hallway, in her thirties bobbed black hair slim figure.
She seemed to frown when she saw both of us standing there.
Good morning, she greeted us with a pleasant smile.

Good morning, Mrs Yudin, I believe.

Yes, that's me.

We have come to see your husband Mr Abel Yudin, is he at home.

Who are you, to begin with.

Sorry Mrs Yudin, I'm detective Grant and my colleague detective Russell, we would like to have a word with your husband about an ongoing enquiry we are looking into.

You better come in, Detective,

With that a young boy came running up the hallway,

Peter goes upstairs, tell your

36

father, he has visitors in the study

"What do they want mummy, "never
mind just "GO Now" enforcing her
instructions,
Come through, have a seat gentleman
can I get you a drink, tea, coffee,
juice.

No, we are fine thanks, the study
seems to house mostly boy's toys,
models of classic cars, helicopters,
a huge TV hung from one wall. a lot
of family photos about on all the
walls, children, mostly, Bob got up
to look at some of the photos of
older generations, some looked like
they were taken perhaps during
wartime, others going way back in
the family history.

Hello gentlemen, my wife tells me
you are detectives

Mr Yudin, was about five feet two or
a bit more, very stocky build
receding hair line, his hands were
snarled and podgy, a pair of working
hands that s for sure, he shook our
hands with a firm grip

Yes, Mr Yudin, I'm detective Grant
this is detective Russell we are
making some enquiries regarding a

cold case from the 2004 a property you owned or had owned come to our attention.

What property would that be detective

A house in Union Street 117

Street, that was sold some years ago, "sorry I'm a bit vague about that I'm not really involved with the properties I own. That's done by Mr Abraham.

But you did own it, is that right

Yes, but I have enough to do running my own company Yudin wholesalers. These properties are a left over from my Father's Day, he enjoyed helping those less fortunate. It's a time-consuming business seeing to all these houses, so I passed on the responsibility to Mr Abraham, he takes care of things.

But you did own that house.

Yes

Would you be aware of who lived in that house, over a period of years?

No, But Mr Abraham will have all those details for you. Can I arrange a time for you to meet him at the office, he will have things at hand to give you the right answers or information?

That would be most helpful, Mr Yudin

When would be convenient, tomorrow after lunch about 2pm

That's fine, can you give us the office address and contact details,

Here is my card, with the address and phone numbers, Mr Abraham has a small office at the rear of the warehouse, blue door, can you give me any information what's this about.

Well, no, we are just trying to discover who was living there, at the time, it may, or may not help us with our enquiries at this stage. It has only recently come to our attention; the house might have been used by criminals.
Once we have a word with Mr Abraham, we may have more of an idea, we may still come back to talk to you, Mr Yudin.

Well, if you need to talk to me

again, I'm up and at work by four am
at the Meat Markets, best time for
me is late afternoon.

It would not be that early, that's
for sure, Jim reassured him with a
smile, as they got up to leave.
I notice you have lot of old German
family photos. Your dad had a sense
of humour.

Abel looked at the Detective, what
makes you say that.

The Anagram of Ragmen is German,
hence German tailor. He must have
been a proud man.

He was, yes.

Well thanks again Mr Yudin.

Glad to have been of some assistance
Detective.

The boy we saw earlier, was standing
by the front door entrance as we
approached, he opened the door for
us, "thank you, young man".

Your most welcome, he said with a
smile.

40

CHAPTER 6

Back at the station, it seemed all
go there, more notes pinned to the
work board, conformation of past
owners, up to present day.
Two well suited people could be seen
in the governor's office.
Two Americans from the American
Embassy got wind of the sudden
interest in the old case, whispered
Danny Addis from behind his computer
screen.
A knock on the office window
indicating, for us to go inside, the
two Americans turned to see who we
were, Come in shut the door
These are detective Russell and
detective Grant, the Americans
leaned over to shake our hands,
This gentleman is from the American
Embassy Mr Clyde Baker, and Miss Val
Smith. Enquiring about these new
developments in the case of Rebecca
Finklestein.
I've shared with them what little we
have turned up at present
but until something more positive
and relevant to the case, comes to
light. They will wait for a report
from us before contacting their
Justice Department.

Yes, a lot of wasted man hours last time, with no results, said Mr Baker, we hope we have better luck this time, poor girl.

Thanks for your time Chief Inspector, Mr Baker said as he, and Miss Smith left.

Right how did you get on with the previous owner.

Very good we have a meeting with his property manager tomorrow afternoon.

Contact that Mr Khan see if you can pay him another visit before you have that meeting in the afternoon, have a look around the property see the lay of the land, check the garden area

Yes gov.

"Carol, how did you get on with the neighbours in union street.

Not a lot, apparently everyone I spoke to say a single guy, who came and went, but never lived there as such. thought he was doing work there.

42

Addis you and lusty go over to the library, if she borrowed books she might have also gone on their computers, see what you can find out.

Abel Yudin could be heard shouting in his study, what the bloody hell is going on Henry, I've had two detectives here today, about the house in Union Street,117, you sold it a couple of years ago. I've arranged a meeting for you, with the detectives tomorrow at 2pm, make sure all the details are in order. Have Daniel there with you, he knows more than you with these houses.

Hello Mr Khan, thanks for seeing us again, would you mind if we have a walk through, and around the house we would like to have a closer look at the garden.

"Not at all, where would you like to start.

Just like to go over your statement once more

When you viewed the property, what was in this room.

Just a kitchen chair nothing else,

43

oh yes, a window blind.

Dining room

Empty, there was an old sheet pinned
over the window.

Was there much in the kitchen.

Yes, a lot of empty milk cartons 4
Pinter's, also black bags full of
empty fast-food containers etc.

Hallway

Pretty clear, just junk mail stuff

Upstairs, bathroom.

Yes, a few things, soap, toothpaste,
towels, toilet rolls
that sort of stuff

Box room

Empty again

Front bedroom.

Empty old curtains up at the window
that's it

Back bedroom

44

That is where all the items were

Right so not a lot, apart from this room, can we have a look at the garden Mr Khan.

Mostly grassed over, veg patch children's swing

Your, veg patch,

NO, NO, the same as when we moved in, we just sit out on the patio. not really into gardening

I think we might look at that area, Mr Khan.

How do you mean, like dig it up?

Yes, I would like some of our men in here just to rule out any suspicions. Well Mr Khan we believe a young girl was in this house, before you moved in, subsequently she became a missing person, we just need to clear up all avenues of our investigation.
"I do hope it's a wasted exercise Detective, Poor girl.

Grant and Addis were led to the

45

chief librarian's office.
Good morning, Mrs Alexander, I'm detective Grant and this is detective Addis, I believe you have already spoken to Detective Russell about book details we were interested in. You gave us the name of the last borrower of the book.

Yes, that's right. Was it of any help to you.

Yes, indeed, we have a few more questions we would like to ask you if you can help us. We see you have computers here, like most libraries would you have kept a log of the people who used them.

No that would be impossible, people can come in off the street, pay for the use of computer, we then give them a code to log in.

Yes, your right there, Addis said but we should see some record on the hard drive.

Computers are not my best friend; my mobile is enough to get on with.

Grant interjected, that Addis would be the man to find what we are looking for on your computers.

I will have to have a word with my superiors, to get permission.

Who would, that be Mrs Alexander.

That is Mr Stringer, the overall head man of all the departments.

Can you give us his contact details, so we can arrange to get into your computer's?

I can call him now for you.

That would be most helpful.

I will put the Detective on Mr Stringer.

Hello Sir, I'm Detective Grant we are carrying out an investigation into the disappearance of a young lady who was a member of this Library, we would like to investigate the computer's here to see if we can trace any possible movements, we believe she may have used the computers, it would be very helpful.

What would that require, will it stop the library using them.

We are looking at a small window of time, so we could download a copy of the hard drives of the computer's it will be mostly Emails to see if she contacted anyone. The library will not be inconvenienced, also we understand from Mrs Alexander your previous public computer is used in the office, we will also require downloading from those machines.

Yes, that will be fine Detective, just arrange with Mrs Alexander. May I have a word with her.

Mrs Alexander took the phone; she had a word with Mr Stringer. then That is in order, Detective, when would you like to do this gentleman

I can start now, if any of the computers are not in use.

These first two are not in use, I will put Out of order notices on those two screens.

Great I will get my equipment. Addis set up his portable hard drives, to download all the info they may need. Thank you, Mrs Alexander we think, we have covered everything, once we have checked all the information, they will be wiped clean.

I think we have time for a bite to
eat and a pint, before we go off to
see Mr Abraham, Addis.

I'll go an order some drinks while
you put your gear away.

Rose & Crown small pub with big menu
outside, two pints of light & bitter,
what sandwich's do you have.

Cheese, Ham, Chicken, Or our special
Ploughman's.

Two Ploughman's sounds good.

I will bring them over Gents.

Do you think we will find anything
off these Computers Grant asked
Addis?

Wellbeing they are public Computers
I would hope so, unless she was
really computer savvy and coded the
Emails, which I doubt, then you must
hope that she even used them.

How come you got into all this
computer stuff.

I went on to study at UNI. it's the

49

thing of the future.

Give me a note book any time Grant commented.

Right, I'm going back to the station to see if I can raise any trace of this girl. Your off to see Mr Abraham.

Yes, just need to pick up my car, when we get to the station.

Mr Abraham's office laid behind the main factory building, the blue doorway to Yudin Properties. Quite small office with a reception area, a young lady busy typing away.

Can I help you, the receptionist asked, smiling as she looked up?

Yes, I have an appointment with Mr Abraham, I am Detective Inspector Grant.

That's right, he is expecting you, we don't get many Detectives in here, again smiling broadly. She knocked and opened the office door, to announce I had arrived. Go in sir, she indicated with her hand.

Good afternoon, Mr Abraham, I'm
Detective Inspector Grant

Good afternoon, Detective this is my
son Daniel, how may we help you. Mr
Yudin. told me you were looking for
information on Union Street, house,
that we had on our books at one time.

Mr Abraham looked old school; pin
stripped three-piece suit heavy
built, serious type of mannerism but
seemed a tad nervous Perhaps Yudin
would not be too pleased with the
police sniffing around his business
premises.
His son looked even more suspect,
seemed to avoid eye contact for some
reason, would not like to meet him
on a dark night, straggly hair
looked like it could do with a good
wash, chin stubble. did not seem to
fit in an office situation. I
suppose it was his family duty. One
day he may well be running this side
of Mr Yudin's business.

We are carrying out some enquiries
regarding a house in Union Street
number 117, we spoke to Mr Yudin who
owned the house, he informed us that
you dealt with the property.

Yes, I dealt with that part of his

51

company, dealing with sales and letting's.
Mr Yudin phoned me to tell me get out all the details you required on the house.
Daniel is more hands on regarding the day to day running of the houses.

Who was the last tenant, can you give me start and finish dates, also the previous tenant. Can you give me some background on them please?

Mr& Mrs O'Shea, they were there for just over 10 years.
Very nice couple, middle aged, kept the house in good order. I believe they were an Irish couple; they often went over to Ireland for holidays quite regularly.
The next tenants were, Mr& Mrs Young, a young couple who were both working and saving to buy their first house.

Do you have their forwarding address by any chance?

Yes, we always ask for them, in case any problems with the final readings of the utilities. But I'm not sure if they would be current, after all this time. The O'Shea's gave us a contact address in Ireland. That's that one. Mrs Young gave us her

mother's address, as they were
moving in with her to help with
their savings.

Thanks for those we will check them
out.
I see that the house was empty for
two years, was there a reason for
that, lying empty.

Yes, the house needed to be up
graded, also there was rumours that
the Council were making plans for re
developing that area, so we waited,
then decided to sell after they
changed their minds on the redevelopment.
Everything was above board, as it
should be, it was sold to a Mr Khan.

Your more hands-on Daniel, what was
your roll in the company.

I would organise any repairs to be
carried out on the houses, he
answered, whist sorting paperwork
without looking up. If they had any
questions, I was their first point
of contact.

What was the house like prior to the
sale.

Empty, we tidied up the gardens

53

mostly, cut the grass Rooms were
empty just the odd things here and
there.

Do you remember a single bed in the
rear bedroom?

Not off hand, as I said, it was sold
as seen, maybe a bed was there. Not
too sure After being empty for that
period we checked for squatters had
not broken in, all utilities had
been shut off any way

Right, I think I have enough details
for now, if I have any more
questions I will get back in touch.
Can you give me this office phone
number in case we need to call you,
also your home address and phone
numbers?

Is that necessary Detective.

Standard practise I'm afraid, not
like yourselves, we work out of
hours quite frequently.

Thank you, Detective we are pleased
to help, Henry interjected, just
call Daniel, as I said he is more
hands on. Daniel looked at his
father, but managed a slight smile

CHAPTER 7

Bob Grant. got back to the station,
everyone seemed to be in the one
area of the office, the chief came
out to speak to them all,

Right listen up everyone, Scotland
Yard have decided to put a forensic
team in due to our information we
have gathered, From, Union Street,
to go over the garden areas with a
fine-tooth comb. Good work keeps it
up everyone
Has anyone found out where the
Kaufman family are living.

Yes, Gov we believe they are in
Essex, we are checking the list out.
Russell, you go over to Union Street,
keep with the forensic team see what
they can turn up.

I have got previous tenants
addresses Gov; Carol informed him.

Make a start on that Carol, see if
we can eliminate them from the
enquiry.

Abel Yudin strolled into the small office, still wearing his works apron covered in the evidence of cutting up carcases in the warehouse. How did it go with the Police Henry?

OK they just wanted dates and tenant's names, nothing to worry about Mr Yudin.

Was there a reason to worry then?

No, I was just saying

Just as well, I knew you would have it covered, you alright Daniel.

Yes, good Mr Yudin

Daniel kept his head down, not a lover of Yudin, finds him too volatile, abrasive confrontational at times.

Addis, seemed in his own little world, scrolling the screen of his computer, page upon page of data seemed to just whiz by but I'm sure he knew what he was looking for, even though an onlooker would be hard pressed, to even glimpse any readable words.

Chief I think we may have found Mr Kaufman, address in Essex just going over to have a chat.

Take Bob with you, Jim. see if we can get any more info from him, that he might now remember, after all this time.

Mr Lewinsohn seems to have downsized a bit from Woodside grange road, still big, but not so imposing. Parked cars indicated that someone was at home

Good afternoon, Mr Kaufman, I'm detective Grant and this is Detective Russell.

Yes, what can I do for you.
.
We would like to have a talk with you regarding Rebecca Finklestein.

That was years ago.

We are aware of that, but some new evidence has come to light that may at last clear this case up. May we come in.

Certainly, come in, it would be good to hear about, any new developments.

57

Go through to the lounge, take a seat. What would you like to know.

Can we go over your initial statement at the time of Rebecca's disappearance.

You stated that you had left the house before her

Yes, she never generally got up early.

What time did you leave?

About seven thirty

Was that your normal time for going to work.

No, I generally leave about eight thirty, nine.

Was there a reason you left early that day?

I was expecting a delivery, that's why I left a bit earlier.

Are you still in the same business Mr Lewinsohn.

Yes, still running my Tailoring

business.

You said in your statement you met
Rebecca Finkelstein in New York.

Yes, I was out for the evening, she
obviously heard my accent, she asked
me where I was from. I told her I
was there on business, from London.
Anyway, she said she was looking to
visit London quite soon. I offered
her my business card, if she ever
came over. I told her to contact me.

How long between that meeting, until
you had contact again with her?

About ten days

How did that meeting come about?

She phoned me from the Airport, when
she landed at Heathrow.

Were you surprised by this?

Yes, she caught me off guard, as she
had not been to London before I
invited her to come to our house, as
a temporary measure, until she could
get herself sorted out.

How do you mean caught you off guard?
From what.

Well, not getting the OK from my
wife, to invite her to the house.

How did your wife react to a
stranger moving in with you and the
family?

At first, she was a bit taken aback,
but when she met her, she suggested
she could stay for a short while.
She would be company for Chloe.

How long was she living with you up
to her disappearance.

Just under two weeks.

So, when you left early that day, it
was the last time you saw her.

Yes, all but for that early delivery,
it might have been different.

Your wife's statement suggested,
perhaps you had an unhealthy
interest in the girl. By the way you
kept looking at her, at one point
you were found in her room. How do
you explain that?
His face flushed slightly

She was asking about work in the

area.

What did she do all day, if she was not working, did she use a computer here?

Not as far as I know. She never even had a mobile phone at the time My daughter gave her an old one of hers to use.

I must ask you, were you involved in a relationship with this girl.

ABSOLUTELY NOT. I was just helping her whilst she was here. A good Samaritan if you will.

Just one last question Mr Kaufman, you moved to a new house soon after she disappeared, was there a reason for that.

Well six months, I think was not that soon.

I can assure you; it raised a few eyebrows at the time. A young girl disappears, you then move away, seems odd to me.

This new evidence, you have, it's only now come to light. Can you give me an idea what that might be?

We are not at liberty to disclose that Mr Kaufman.

That's a shame, how long do you think it will be before it's solved.

Thanks for your time, I think that will be all for the moment.

Here is my business card, with my details, anytime you want to speak to me I'm here for Rebecca.

What do you think of him Bob.?

Not too sure, he comes across as concerned, perhaps too concerned do you think.

Do you think he could be involved then?

He could be, but for what reason.

Midlife crisis, younger women, got rejected, who knows.

It would not be the first time, or the last.

CHAPTER 8

The Forensic team had moved into
Union Street, they had brought in a
Ground Penetrating Radar machine, to
check the garden areas, for earth
disturbances. Mr Khan looked on with
great interest
Mr Khan was watching all the goings
on from his upstairs bedroom window.
As the radar machine went back and
forth. A group of men were looking
at some charts that had been printed
out some head shaking, as they
checked them.
A loud knocking at the front door
startled Mr Khan out of his
concentration. He ran down the
stairs to find a policeman there.

Sorry to trouble you sir. The
detective outside would like a word.

Certainly. As he stepped outside
thinking he would get, close to all
the action.

Mr Khan Was the veg plot there when
you moved in, or did you dig it over
Detective Russell enquired.

No, it was there when we moved in, I
kept meaning to get it turfed over,
but it was not top of the list of

63

things to do.

We may have to check it out, a small amount of digging might be involved. Have you at any time dug it up at all, whilst you have been here.

No just took the weeds out.

Thank Mr Khan the constable will show you back to the house

Reluctantly, Mr Khan returned to the inside once again.

Addis How long are you going to be with those computers any useful leads we can work with Vincent, barked across the squad room. I thought computers were fast, suppose to save people lots of time.

They are, I'm narrowing to the ones of interest, quite a lot of rubbish on here, opens your eyes to see what people write about. Hopefully I may have something shortly

I want anything interesting pinned on the work board. Carol did you speak to the Americans about the girl, had they managed to find out anything new on the passport she had.

No Sir, as you know it was
counterfeit, not been able to find
out anything further.

One step forward two back, hope
those forensic team comes good
Your phone's ringing Gov, Addis
shouted.

HELLO, Vince rasped, Hi Jim what's
going on

OK right. I will be straight down
thanks

Looks like we may have a something
Lads, I'm off to see what they have
come up with.

Alright Jim have they good news for
us.

It would seem a body is buried in
the Veg plot; they have sent for S O
C O Before it is removed.

They walked into the back garden,
which was now taped off crime scene.
A tent covered the relevant grave
site.
The forensic team were, at the end

of this part of the process, until they get back to the lab, to carry out Post-mortem.

Hello Vincent said Helen, not a lot to go on. Body covered in sheeting and plastic I will get a report done by the morning for you.

Thanks Helen.

Russell, go back to the station, inform the others, on the new developments, we will have to do a re- assessment of our case, from missing to murder. I will see you in the morning.

GOOD MORNING, everyone, as you now know, we have Another added mystery on our hands, A body has been found, so this is now a murder inquiry we don't know a lot at this stage, until the pathologist can give us some info on cause of death of Rebecca Finklestein or why. So now we are working on the assumption, that this was the reason for the abduction.
Excuse me Gov, Addis said as he went into his office. I think we may also have something off the computer, it

seems she had used the machine in the library.

That's good we needed a break in this bloody case, what have you found out.

You will have to bear with me, look these are some of the Email address that looked a bit iffy, what I done I tried each address with an Anagram tool, a lot of the addresses used, were a jumble of letters.
So, I tried it, people use it to disguise their identities

That seemed to work, when I got to this one Feline-skint@hotmail.com Turned out to be the Anagram of Rebecca so perhaps Rebecca Frankenstein did this for anonymity, in case someone was stalking her, or she was hiding. It went to an Email address in America, Brooklyn to be Precise.

That's great Dan, anything else.

I translated the Email, it reads I want to come home Papa? Can you come for me please Soon. I miss you so much, please let me know Quickly.

67

lots of love, as ever.

Do we know who this was sent to.

I would guess her father, it's
another odd-looking Email address.
You would need someone at the other
end to do some digging around, to
see who is using it at that end. Its
Radjackle@hotmail.com

OK Addis, well done.
I will talk to the Yanks about these
Emails.

Can I speak to Mr Clyde Baker please,
I am Detective Chief Inspector
Vincent Lusty

One moment sir, I will put you
through.

Hello Clyde, this is Vincent Lusty

Hi, Vince, how are things going.

We have a few more leads on the
Rebecca Finklestein. We recovered a
body from a house, we believe she
was kept at.

You found her body Vince, that is
very welcome, but sad news after all
this time. I'm taken aback by that.

Can you come over to the station, I
will fill you in, there are some
things you may be able to help us
with from your end.

No problem, Inspector, I will drop
by after lunch, I have a prior
meeting before that. OK.

That will be good, see you then.

Come in Clyde, looks like Rebecca
Finklestein was at the address we
were looking at. Also, more
importantly she used a computer at
her local library as well. She sent
an email to someone; we believe to
be her father. Apparently, the email
addresses were new, only they are in
a code, says my computer geek. The
correspondence was with someone in
New York, Brooklyn as far as we can
ascertain, I'll give you the
addresses can you have a look at
your end for us.

Yes, that would be a simple job I'll
get them sent of once I'm back at my
office. Anything else going down.

We have now recovered her body from
the address we were searching.

Excuse me Sir, you've been asked to go down to the lab.

You can come with me Clyde if you like.

Sure thing.

The Body lay on the slab, sheeted over. Doctor Nicol doing her notes on the test results.

Good morning, gentlemen, how are you Vincent.

I hope a lot better now you have called me down here. This is Mr Clyde Baker from the American Embassy who has an interest. in this case This Dr Helen Nicol our Pathologist who saves our skins in a lot of cases putting us on the right track. Well, what's the synopsis Helen.

Firstly, death through a broken neck, a clean break.

Did she put up a fight Helen, any defensive wounds.

WOW, WOW. HANG ON THERE. No defensive wounds, a clean break to

70

the neck, it would have been instant.
But this is a young male mid-
twenties. Not a she at all.

Vincent and Clyde looked at each
other in A bemused fashion at the
revelation they had still not found
Rebecca. But who was he then. what
part of this puzzle does he fit into

A HE. Why did you not say something
before?

Remember the body was wrapped up
with sheeting, we only saw the top
of the skull indicating it was a
Body A human. rather than someone
burying a family pet. So, he was
removed very carefully, so we did
not lose anything by opening the
wrapping on site, a more contained
removal in the Lab. My theory at
this stage, someone from behind
snapped his neck, a very clean break,
no other signs on the body no marks
or injuries. No defensive wounds
Except a Star of David Tattoo with
the initials H V R. That's it

Excuse me Helen may I look at the
Tattoo Baker requested

Yes, come over, the Pathologist
lifted the side of the sheet

71

exposing the faded Tattoo on what
was left of his right ankle she
handed him a magnifying glass as I
said, the Body was well on the way
of decomposing completely, no facial
features discernible for
identification purposes.

I have seen this Tattoo before, any
luck with prints of any kind

Just a partial, one finger That's
the best we could do.
Also, we have what looks like part
of a phone number the middle section
numbers are gone but the remaining
ones are very, very faint you may
need to work on that. That was found
in the corner of his jeans pocket,
again what was left of them.
In Another couple of months, we
might not have got so much as what
we have now.
I will finish my report and send it
up with the photos.

Thanks Helen

Nice to meet you Mr Baker

likewise giving her a broad smile.

CHAPTER 9

Come back up to the office Clyde, I
will give you those email addresses

Can I also get copies of the photos
especially the Tattoo and Phone
number when you have them? That
tattoo Looks familiar as well.

Yes, as soon as I get them, I will
send them over

Well, this has been a fruitful day
for both of us,
How did you get rolling with this
case, we had very little success
when we were investigating way back
when? Then out of the blue all these
years later, you're nearly solving
the case

Vincent got up to retrieve a book in
the plastic bag put it on the desk
to show Clyde This is what started
it all, an old Professor walked into
a police station with this book
Grimm's Fairy Tales he got from an
auction house a little while back,
he was fretting over what he saw
inside on one of the pages, written
by Rebecca Finklestein pleading for
help
He said it was a gut feeling that it

was genuine, not some silly prank that kids do,
We had a quiet day, so I sent Jim Russell to investigate it. It's now called from there to where we are at now, more fortuitous luck then judgement.

It's strange sometimes how things develop on cases also that tips come in anonymously that gets things moving in the right direction Vince.

Sure does, I will get that stuff sent over.

Thanks for the update, Vince.

Jim when you talk with Daniel Abraham, make sure to bring his computer and tablets, or whatever. make sure he has his mobile with him.

I'LL do that Gov

Right take Addis with you Jim he may know what to bring back.

The flat was part of a very large old house, obviously turned into flats years ago, after these buildings stood empty for a while, cost effective, for this large place Families could no longer afford to

run them. Was this one of Yudin's
many properties. It was surely down
at the lower end of the market going
by the outside wheelie bins all over
the place A long row of bells and
names by the front entrance. The
hallway in had some bikes propped to
one side, Daniel Abraham was flat
one, saved us the walk up all those
stairs.
At least he was home going by the
music we could hear we banged on the
door after no response from the Bell.
Eventually the door opened Obviously
been in the shower when we rang as
he stood there in his bath robe Mr
Daniel Abraham

Yes, looking a little concerned

I'm Detective Russell and this is
Detective Addis, I believe you spoke
to a colleague of ours regarding a
house in Union Street Finchley

It was my father that spoke to him,
I just work there.

Well Sir we would like you to come
to the station to answer some
further questions

Why me, what about my father

We are not sure at this stage we
believe you had a more hands on
approach regarding the property

Can this not be done another time I
have things on tonight surely
another day would not hurt
I'm afraid not, we also need to take
your computers Etc

You are joking That's my personal
property nothing to do with the
business

Therefore, we need it, what sort of
computers do you have asked Addis, I
see you have a desktop tower do you
have a laptop or tablet

I have all three

We will take all of those with us

Why did you not take the computer
from the office?

If need be, we will

This seems a lot of trouble over the
house in Union Street

That may well be Sir, but things
have moved on since then. It will be
explained to you when we get back to

the station.

Do I need to take anything else with me? Am I under arrest

No, you're not under arrest you are just assisting us in some more details that have come up, just your coat then we can get going Then the sooner its done, the sooner you get home.

Returning to the station, they seemed to go their own ways Addis taking the computers over to his workstation to see what little secrets Daniel Abraham might be hiding. Mobile first the easy one to check through. Tinder, plenty more fish, and a few I did not know typical lads sex dating sites snap-chat, twitter, he had them all.

Daniel was led into an interview room; Lusty was already seated going over the case files.

Hello Mr Abraham, take a seat glad you decided to come in to assist us

I had no choice did I, you've taken my computers and my mobile

I think your mobile will be back

with you quite soon so don't worry,
now things have changed quite
significantly since you were last
spoken with.
You stated before that you knew very
little about Union Street since it
was vacated other than keeping it
under review in the case that
squatters may move in is that
correct

Yes, as I said before

You also said you tidied up the
Garden area, did you notice any
change or difference in the Garden,
The Veg patch for instance.

As I said before we tied up any
rubbish from the Garden

What sort of rubbish was that

How would I know, it was just
rubbish sweet wrappers old papers,
cans, that sort of things?

Did you do any work on the Veg patch

Do I look like a gardener?

So, you have no Idea then that
someone was secretly living there

Not to my knowledge. sometimes I
just drove past I didn't all ways go
in.

We believe a Girl called Rebecca
Finklestein was in that house do you
know her

Was that the Girl that disappeared,
I remember That at one time.

Yes, you do know something then

NO, NO. I read that in the papers.

Whilst searching the house we have
found a Dead Body.

Daniel's face froze his eyes flicked
from side to side his brain now in
overdrive.

Do you know how it got there Daniel;
he shook his head which was now
lowered towards the table?
You don't seem to be surprised
Daniel, what else do you know that
you're not telling us. It would be
better to get it off your mind and
tell us what you done Daniel.
Denial won't help you. just tell us
it was an accident, or something
happened, you didn't mean to do it.

79

Daniel what are you thinking come on lad

NO Comment. I WANT A SOLICITOR

Is this your way of dealing with its Daniel?

I WANT A SOLICITOR

We will arrange a solicitor for you, or do you have your own Solicitor
Can I phone my father, he will know who to call?

We will have to book you in Daniel, so we can carry on with our investigation's
Constable takes Mr Abraham to the desk Sargent to book him in on suspicion of Murder.
When that's done let Mr Abraham make a phone call to his father to arrange a Solicitor,

Back to the Squad room, well lads looks like we have a suspect in custody. So, we need to put everything we must put a good case together.
Addis How you are getting on with those computers, Mobile was clean but downloaded all that was on it, I'm sure the tablet was used for

things you don't want anyone else to
see by what I'm seeing.
Here is An American site with the
initials H V R

Show me that Dan, that looks like
the Tattoo from our Body, now we can
connect Abraham's with the Body we
just need a name.
The initials stand for Holocaust
Victims Revenge
Have you tried the numbers we have
for the mobile Dan?

I think it is a UK number they start
with 07 it will be a case of finding
the number with the same numbers,
like a crossword solver. That can
throw up several number combinations
calculation could be quite a few.

Yes, I think whoever he is. he is
not going without a fight keep at it,
Dan.

It was not long before old man
Abraham's arrived with a solicitor
in tow. Part of HYMENS, SAMPSON &
GOLBERG. One of the biggest law
firms, with an aggressive approach
with all things Jewish. So much so
that Mr Ariel Sampson was here
rather than a junior flunky, but
Abraham's would also have some clout.

The desk Sargent had sent for
Vincent, to come down to see his
visiting party

Good to see you Mr Sampson as they
were acquainted from over the years
and Mr Abraham.

I wish to have a consultation with
my client Daniel Abraham,

Yes, we are just sorting an office
you can use, Mr Abraham I'm afraid
you will not be able to attend that
for obvious reasons, if you would
like to wait in the waiting room,

Abraham gave a nod come this way Mr
Sampson I will take you through have
a seat in there we will bring Daniel
through

Right Daniel, your Solicitor is here
to talk with you as they led him
into a small interview room,
Hello Daniel, you've met me before

Yes, but not directly is my father
coming
Yes, he is here but for legal
reasons you cannot see him until you
have made a formal statement of the
facts to the police.
You better give me your version of

82

the facts, truthful facts Daniel
this is a serious Charge that will
have devastating consequences if
your found to be guilty

I'M NOT GUILTY

THAT'S a good start, but I must
stress Daniel if you are guilty You
Must Confide in Me, So I can help
you is that understood

YES, YES, I'M NOT GUILTY

Well, we are off to a good start
then I believe you.

It was nearly an hour before Mr
Sampson came out to speak to
Detective Russell

Do you have any hard evidence
against my client detective?

Not yet we will be looking to Daniel
to make a full statement on the
matter now you are here. I will
bring in Detective Lusty. We will be
recording this interview, all that
are present are Mr Daniel Abraham
the accused, Mr Ariel Sampson
solicitor for Daniel Abraham
Detective Jim Russell Myself Chief
inspector Vincent Lusty time now is

83

14.25 Tuesday the 12/11/2014

Can you state your full name?

Daniel Abraham

You have been brought in for questioning regarding the discovery of a body in the garden of 117 Union Street Finchley Our forensic team indicate the time of Death, would put it at the time you owned the property

What date are we talking here Detectives?

Approximately giving a window either side to be 2004

Daniel, do you know anything about that or how it got there

Looking at his Solicitor replying to NO.

Were you responsible for the death or killing of this person.

Frustratingly NO, NO, I never Killed Him.

Mr Sampson indicating to Daniel to calm himself

84

Now that is very interesting Daniel,
very interesting indeed. How did you
know it was a male we were talking
about?

NO COMMENT

Do you know the name of the This
Victim?

NO COMMENT

That would indicate you know more
than what your prepared to say
Daniel

NO COMMENT

We had not mentioned a male was
involved, we were asking you about a
missing girl, Rebecca Finklestein at
no time did we ask you about a male

NO COMMENT

We have some evidence that you did
know him from information on your
Tablet.

NO COMMENT

I believe you knew him, you argued
with him Then killed him and buried

85

him in the garden

NO COMMENT

Showing Daniel, a photo of a Tattoo, have you seen this symbol before

NO COMMENT.

We will call an end to the interview now 15,10

Detective Lusty, are you charging my client.

No, we still have on going enquiries being made.

I suggest we are out of here until you can come up with more convincing evidence that my client was involved with this Murder.
Have you finished with his computers?

Not at this stage, we are still looking at them. But Mr Abraham can have his Mobile phone back.

Thank you, Gentlemen,

CHAPTER 10

Well, that went well Jim. We need

some other leads This Case needs to
come up with something. If we are
going to crack this. Let's hope the
Yanks can come up with some thing
Daniel, Daniel what have you done
said Mr Abraham said as he greeted
his son. Tell me this cannot be true.
No Father it is not true you can be
assured.
Daniel, you come to my office in the
morning we will go over all the
facts to put them in order. so, when
the Police wish to speak again,
which they will, we can have the
facts right, as you know them.
I will leave your father to take you
home.

Thank you, Mr Sampson, for all your
help, I will see you in the morning.

Have we any idea yet who the victim
is

No Gov very little from the body,
only fragments of clothing and
trainers

Has anyone gone back to check on
missing persons from that date

Yes Gov. we are searching through
all records

Addis how are doing with the computers

Working my way through the stuff

look, have a look at the photo of the partial mobile number, give it a shot to see if we can get the missing numbers some how

A big ask that, it could be into hundreds of permutations, so don't hold your breath.

I'm going down to see the Pathologist, someone surely can come up with some god news for me.
Hello Helen, That John Doe we brought in, can you get his DNA, OR Blood type to help this case along, we could get it on the data base, I have extracted some bone marrow that has been sent off once its back I will let you know.
Have you made any headway elsewhere Vincent

We are bringing in someone of interest Daniel Abraham he seems to be a bit evasive last time. Going to see if we can get him to cough up something, lean on him a bit harder, to help us.

Hello Daniel, Vincent said, in a low welcoming manner, trying a different tact, to see if we can get the information we are looking for.

Is Mr Sampson here yet.

I believe he will be here shortly; would you mind just answering a few questions until he arrives.

That won't be necessary Daniel, Mr Sampson said as he entered the room, Inspector you know better than to ask that without my presence. Now we can begin if your ready Inspector.

I'm turning on the recording machine It's now 11.23, I'm Detective Vincent Lusty Also Detective Jim Russell, with Daniel Abraham, and Mr Ariel Sampson Solicitor. all parties acknowledge their names for the recording.
Just going over the last time we spoke to you Daniel, you indicated that you were innocent of the accusations, regarding the body found in the garden of the house your company owned.
Is that still the case?

Addis knocked as he partly entered the interview room,

Excuse me Sir, can we have a word outside.

11.40 recording stopped Vincent Lusty leaving the interview room.

What's up Dan.

You know those Emails I showed you from the library computers, well that Email address is on Daniel Abraham's Tablet. So, he has a connection with Rebecca Finklestein. Also, he was heavily into an extreme far right Jewish group. His tablet is full of their indoctrinating bile.

That's bloody great Dan, we will see what he says about that, good work Dan.

Vincent Lusty re-entering interview room 11.51, confirming name and time. Turning on recorder, Vincent Lusty returning to interview.

I asked you a question Mr Abraham is that still the case.

Yes, I never committed any Murder.

I will ask you something apart from

the murder.
What was your relationship with
Rebecca Finklestein.

I never had a relationship with her

Are you sure, Are you quite sure

Yes, I am sure

Can you explain why this Email
address (showing Mr Abraham copy of
email address) is on your computer
Daniel. If you don't know her.

He looks at Mr Sampson No Comment

In that Email Daniel, is your post
code, and house number, also the
word Traitor 2004. What can you tell
me about that?

NO COMMENT

We also found on your computer,
several extreme Far right sites that
preach violence for their idolatry
solution.

NO COMMENT

Inspector can I have some time with
my client. Before we proceed, owing

91

to this new information you have,
brought to our attention

Interview now Stopped at. 12.05
We can stop for lunch Mr Sampson.
will that be sufficient time, we
will continue again at 14.30 hrs.

Yes, that would be convenient
Inspector.

I would express to your client to
tell us all he knows. Due to
information, we are now uncovering,
and subsequent findings. it would be
in his best interest.

Inspector we are ready to continue
now.

Switching on recording machine,
those present are, Mr Ariel Sampson,
Solicitor, Mr Daniel Abraham. Also,
detective James Russell, myself
Detective Inspector Vincent Lusty.

Before you start questioning Mr
Abraham, I have a statement to make
regarding your enquiries on this
Matter.
I have had instructions from Mr
Abraham. That he will give you all
the help he can. Furthermore, he is
willing to answer any of your

questions on this matter.

Thank you, Mr Sampson. I will again
ask, Daniel did you murder the
person, we removed from the garden
ground at 117 Union Street Finchley

He lifted his head now, looking at
the two Detectives.

NO, I did not kill this person.

Did you bury, or have any
involvement in burying the body in
the garden

NO. I did not bury or help anyone
else to bury this person.

Are you prepared to inform us, of
anything about this case? That would
help our inquiries.

Yes, I am.

Well, why don't you start at the
beginning of your known evolvement
Because we believe, you are involved
big time Daniel.

Inspector do you think we could get
a Tea or Coffee.

Yes. Constable, can we get some

drinks in. Yes Sir

When you're ready Daniel.

It was just by chance, as I said
before, I periodically checked the
house for squatters or break ins.
When I went in, I sensed that
someone was in the house, I heard a
noise upstairs I went up to see what
was going on. I looked in the front
Main bedroom nothing. Checking the
Box room, I heard a noise behind me.
I saw a man standing by the top of
the stairs, stopping anyone from
going down.
I asked him who he was, as he was
trespassing in my house. With that a
young girl burst out of the bathroom
in front of me, and to the right
side of him
She tried to push past him to get
away, He was looking in my direction
at this time She surprised both of
us, he seemed to be knocked off
balance, his hand missed the
banister as he fell backwards to try
and save himself. It was that quick
he fell backwards hitting his head
on the opposite wall
I heard a crack when his head struck
the wall he never moved or said
anything.
He was laying with his feet on the

top landing his head at a funny
angle.
The girl looked terrified, looking
at me looking at him.

What were you doing at this point.

I just stood there; I asked the Girl
why she was in my house.
She stared at me hard, I don't know
I was brought here, I've been held
captive.
It was then I noticed the handcuff
hanging from her wrist Who has been
holding you captive. Are you being
abused, Is it a Sex ring.

No, she told me, they were going to
kill her.

Kill you WHY! what have you done.

PLEASE HELP ME

So, you are saying this man fell and
died, how did you know he was dead.

He looked dead, I was as frightened
as the girl, I went to check his
pulse, my fear was he would wake up
and grab me, but I needed the key to
the cufflinks, I could not feel a
pulse.

That was a good time to call the police then Daniel, that's what normal people do when there has been an accident. Is that not right Mr Sampson.

Obviously. But my client was in shock at this stage.

Shock or not, why did you not report it, I think you are trying to cover yourself with a far-fetched story, that's more like it Daniel, isn't it?

NO, NO, that is what happened, that is how it happened,
I said I would be truthful, and I am, why won't you believe me. You are trying to make me admit something that is not true. I did not kill this man.

Well so far Daniel you have lied about knowing the girl., Also you have incriminating evidence on your computer which also implicates you, in other ways. You have up to this stage been uncooperative with our enquiries.
As now we are getting closer to the truth, that you killed this man and buried his body in the garden. You were the only one to have access to the property and garden, can you see

where we are coming from Daniel. NOW you give us, this cock and bull story that it was an accident, how convenient.

That only strengthens our resolve, if you say it was an accident you should have reported it, then you would not be sitting here Daniel would you. Let's talk about your Computer Tablet, an Email tells us you contacted someone in the Brooklyn in the USA.

Again, I have not, I don't know anyone in Brooklyn I do not know that Email address.

I thought you said you were going to help us also you were going to be cooperative, in all areas of this investigation.

I'm trying to do that, but you're not believing me.

Yes Daniel, but you must give us solid information, that can be collaborated, and verified with the facts. We cannot just take your word for it, give us something we can confirm with others or evidence that supports what you're saying. You said a girl was there she could back

up your story. Then we might start
to believe you, where is she Daniel.

Daniel looked at the Inspector,
giving a sigh.
I don't know where she is. I keep
telling you.
If I knew where she is, I would tell
you.

Getting back to the scene you
described at the house. You were
going to check the house, for
squatters or break ins, just by
chance, there were two people inside.

That's right, that is how it
happened, no plan, no nothing,
that's what happened, as I keep
saying,

Why did you not phone the police,
and report that the house had been
broken into, before you went inside.
Don't you think that would have been
the more sensible thing to do.

Yes, in hindsight, I wish I had done.

We will take a break now at 16.45.

I will be back shortly.

CHAPTER 11

Vincent decides to have a word with
Helen Nicol about the John Doe

what brings you down here again
Vincent.

Just a question about the injury on
the head of that male victim we
brought in. We have a suspect we are
talking too. He states that the
victim fell backwards from the
landing in an apparently straight
line. Hitting his head directly on
the wall. That's what killed him, is
that possible.

Helen looked at her notes, yes
that's feasible.

I will look at that, what height
would he have been, we need some
measurements to go by

He had trainers on, so I would
suggest he would be around 5.10-
5.11

In a court of Law. Would you say
that it was the cause of death, if
other evidence pointed us in that
direction?

As you know, all things depend on contributors to actual cause or causes. At this stage I can reiterate it is a possibility.

It looks like we will have to dig deeper. To nail him

Right, everyone how are we getting on, found anything that we can use yet.

Addis.

Still going through the computers Gov.

Detective Vincent Lusty returns to interview room at 17.05

Right Daniel let's see if we can clear a few things up, firstly this girl you say was in the house. Where is she now Daniel.

As I said before I do not know.

When we were at the Union Street, she begged me to get her away from the house, there was a second person, she had not seen, but heard them talking when he turned up. I took

100

her to my flat, she even laid on the
floor of the car in case we were
followed.

At last, something, what was her
name

She would not tell me her name, she
said it was better for me that I did
not know, just call me Reba she said.
She asked me to swear not to tell
anyone she was with me. Also, don't
go back to the House, they are
ruthless and would kill me.
They will have discovered him by now.

I asked her who they were, she said
something about H.V.R. I think, then
stopped she would not tell me
anything else.

Then what Daniel. She was in your
flat, why did you not report this to
the police.

I wanted too but she said she will
be gone in two to three days, then I
could do what I wanted, she begged
me, to let her stay, and keep quiet
about what went on.

But someone has died, you cannot
leave a body there.

101

They are very thorough; they will have it cleaned up.

Then I came home one day, and she's gone.

Did she leave anything behind, did she give you a contact number at all?

No, she came with nothing. She left a note saying, "thanks"

That's convenient Daniel. Have you still got the note?

No, I binned it, it was just on a scrap of paper.

We will stop there for today it's now 17.50.

Has anyone come up with some new lead or details we can use.

No Gov, we've checked all the usual stuff, having no name for the deceased has not helped there.

Right Grant you and Oats. I want you to go to Mr Kaufman. house in the morning, interview his wife on her own, also the two children, if they live at home. If not get their addresses and phone numbers. There

are clues out there somewhere just
keep digging.

Addis have you got anything from
that computer yet.

Yes Gov, it has coughed up a lot of
info, Abraham' had deleted several
files of the site called, Holocaust.
Victims. Revenge.
I found it on the Dark WEB. That
ties up with the partial tattoo
H.V.R. found on the victim. This it
seems to be the badge of honour for
their members. They seem to be
violent extremists, who are not
liked by the main Jewish community.
This group stems from the second
world war, set up by relatives and
friends who noticed a pattern with
Some of the victims. Also, how some
Jews and their families seemed to be
immune from persecution, that they
were all going through.
Informing on families to the Nazi's
SS, to save their own skin's. Many
families were wiped out due to their
actions.
According to their web site the
H.V.R was set up to find these
collaborators, and either got rid of
them, or reported them to the Nazi's,
as they had been doing to others.
This group has never given up on the

103

Jew's they are looking for, or their
families, subsequently they have
targeted the next generations down.
According to their site there has
been many successes in finding the
descendants all over the world.
So, I think Mr Peter Abraham is
fully a where what may have happened
to Rebecca Finklestein.

Good work Addis, but we just need
more to charge him. Something that
directly links him to her, and the
body, other than the story he is
giving us now. We need to break him
down somehow.

Excuse me Gov, may I have a word in
your office.

What's on your mind Danny.

I know this might seem at odds with
the way you're thinking. But I think
Abraham is not our man.

YOU DON'T Eh, what's your theory Dan,
DO ENLIGHTEN ME

Well, we know, he was there at the
house, we know he saw a young man
there, he has also admitted that he
had further contact with her.
She said there was a second person,

but never saw him. Neither did he. The stuff on the computer, yes, he downloaded their sites, read up on what they were about, as I have explained just now. There seems to be a lack of contact to this site. No connection I believe like many people, you download a site to see what it's about.

Going by his Emails he never contacted them. He was just curious, by what the girl had partially told him.

Admittedly he seems to have only deleted this site since we spoke to him initially. But I don't think he's the one.

To me, if I was him, I would not have admitted to any of this. The computer sites do not make him a murderer.

Right. ok Dan, who do you think done it, have you an alternative theory about that. You seem to dismiss what we have gathered so far, but you're not giving me any other answers

As you say Gov, keep digging. This is an old case, but that's my personal view.

You go and find Grant, no take Val, the pair of you go back to the

Kaufman household re-interview them, especially the children, go over what they said before and what's being said now.

I will carry on interrogating Abraham's. Got that.

Yes Sir.

Good morning gentlemen are we ready to proceed,

Yes, Inspector, Mr Sampson replied, as did Daniel Abraham.

The time now 10,05 turning on recording machine. I'm Detective Vincent Lusty, with Detective Jim Russell, interviewing Daniel Abraham, along with Mr Abraham's solicitor Mr Ariel Sampson.

A simple question to start Daniel still alright to call you Daniel.

Yes.

Have you or about your body, have any Tattoo's.

Tattoo's, Daniel repeated the question.

NO, None.

Would you object to a search of your body for any Tattoo's.

No.

Would you go with detective Russell next door, to check this out please? Tape stopped 10.15

Detective Russell, and Mr Abraham, return to interview room at 10 30.

Were there any tattoos on Mr Abraham Detective Russell?

No Sir.

I would like to recap, on what you told us yesterday, Daniel. That you entered the house at 117 Union Street, to discover some strangers in the house that should not have been there. Namely a Miss Rebecca Finklestein, also a young man is that correct, who subsequently died at the house, is that what you are saying.

Yes, that is correct, I know I am in trouble for not reporting this. But I did not kill that man, or Miss Rebecca Finklestein.

Mr Sampson, can you add anything more, other than what your clients telling us.

Not really, I have spoken to my client extensively I believe he is telling the truth, and innocent of any crime other than not reporting the death of this unfortunate man. This I feel will result in due course, with him being charged for that offence.

That is all for the moment. We will not be charging you at this stage Daniel. But we will continue with our present line of inquiries.

Good day gentlemen.

CHAPTER 12

Russell, we need to have a briefing with the team to go over the information we have.

Addis, and oats arrive at the Kaufman house to go over previous statements by the family.
Good morning, Mrs Kaufman I'm Detective Addis and this is Detective Oats, may we come in, we

108

would like to go over a few things with you, Regarding Miss Finklestein.

Yes, come in take a seat, now what would you like to know that I have not already told you, this has been going on now for such a long time, will it ever end, this continual questioning.

I'm sure it must be stressful for your family, but I'm sure you would welcome these intrusions to clear up this mystery, if it was your daughter, you would like everything done to solve the crime.

Yes, so what would you like to know. In your original statement you said you never actually saw Rebecca that morning.

Yes, I was in the shower about that time, I heard the front door slam shut.

Where was you Husband, Daughter, Son, in the house.

My husband had left early to go to work, I presume my son, and Daughter were getting ready to go to school or work. That is what occurred, by the time I came down. My cleaner

arrived about this time. It was a
normal day for me.

What was your relationship with
Rebecca like, on a day-to-day basis.

She was a similar in age to my own
daughter, she seemed level-headed,
never spoke of her family, she could
be quiet at times spent most of her
time in her room.

How about your husband, what was his
position, being she was staying with
your family?

He felt a bit awkward at times being
he brought her to our house, he did
enter her room to see how she was
each day.

Did you not think that was strange,
that he was taking such an interest
in her, after all she was an
attractive girl, did you think there
was more to his relationship with
her, than what he let on.

Good grief, you must be scrapping
the barrel, to ask me that. He was
concerned for her being a stranger
here being on her own. No, he had no
ulterior motive, being you asked. Is
that it, I'm finished answering your

110

questions.

Can you give us contact details of your daughter, and Son, Address's phone numbers, we need to talk with them as well? Believe me we are trying to solve this case with as little intrusion for you and your family. Thank you for talking to us, and the details for your children.

Clyde Baker on the phone Gov.

OK, hello Clyde, what can I do for you.

Hi Vince, just letting you know there is a detective coming over from New York. As I said when we were talking to Helen Nicol, I sort of recognized that faded Tattoo, on your John Doe. It seems it is a group of extremists who choose a violent way of punishment for relatives of collaborators from the war days.
I am hoping he will be able to give you some assistance, on that side of things. When he arrives, I will set up a meeting with us, to exchange info, now we've got this far.

Sounds good to me, I'll wait for

your call.

Addis and Oats arrived at the daughter flat about five minutes away from her parents' house, a conversion flat in an old Victorian mansion, but a very nice all-round property in its day.
Oats was hoping the daughter would be at home, it looked like there was life going on in some of the rooms, that they could see from the front drive, still some cars parked.

CHLOE Seckel, Number 3. Hello, came a pleasant voice.

Chloe Seckel, formally Kaufman

Yes, can I help you.

I'm detective oats, with the police department, we would like to have a word with you regarding Rebecca Finklestein.

Oh yes, my mother called just now, I will buzz you in.

A tall dark-haired woman greeted us at the door.

Hello detectives, this is a surprise after all this time, poor Rebecca.

112

It's still ongoing then.

Yes, we never give up Mrs Seckel,
I'm Detective Oats and this is
Detective Addis. We know it's been a
long time, but we are updating on
the enquiries made at the time of
Rebecca's disappearance.
Can you give us some idea, what sort
of girl she was, when she lived with
you?

Not too sure, we were about the same
age she seemed to be worldlier wise
on things than I was, perhaps being
an American had something to do with
it. Other than that, we got on fine.
Did she discuss anything about her
family, you can remember?

Nothing really, she did mention she
had a brother, but that was it she
never seemed to want to discuss
family life or where she lived.
I believe it was New York. We did
talk about boys a bit, just girlie
stuff, pop stars and that sort of
thing. She stayed in her room quite
a lot, either reading or studying, I
don't really know to be truthful. It
wasn't until she disappeared, we
could not tell anyone anything about
her, we simply did not know her,
strange that. I always hoped she

just moved on, got fed up being here, you know the sort of thing us girls get in our heads, when we are young there's always greener pastures. She came to mind over the years, I even thought she might just show up. But then we moved to a new house, she could have returned unknowing to us.

Did she meet any boys whilst she was here?

Yes, she did say she met a nice boy in the Library, Roy I think his name was, I did tell the police at the time.

That's interesting, we would check on that to see if they traced him. Anything else you can add.

Not really.

How did the rest of the family, get on with her?

About the same as me. My brother was a bit keen on her, as boys are at that age, with a new female on the block so to speak.
But no, just normal things.

Well, that's been helpful, gives us an idea to where she was at, at the

114

time. How was your father with her?

Dad was always fussing over her,
keen to know what she was up to,
where she was going If he could help
her with things. I know he showed
her where the library was, she liked
reading.

One other thing, did she use the
internet at all when she was here.
No, either me, or my brother would
be on it, or our mobiles.
I gave her an old phone of mine, as
she said she never had one, That I
thought a bit strange, all my
friends had mobiles. not sure even
if she used that. I put my number in
it, as well as the house number in
case she got lost.

Thanks again Mrs Seckel for your
help. We are going to see your
brother now.

He is away, on business, back on
Sunday, if that's some help.

Yes, saves us a trip.

Not much different from the initial
statement, they really did not know
this girl at all Val.

No, she came and went, like a shadow. I would presume the brother will be much the same going by what Mrs Seckel's said.

Everyone in the office were going over all the bits of information trying to build a picture of events.

How did you get on with Mrs Kaufman Val?

Not gleaned anything we didn't know already Gov, the daughter was the same, the son is away now, should catch him next week, when he's home.

Tell you what Addis contact Daniel Abraham tell him we have finished with his computers, see if he wants to pick it up.

Helen called me I will catch you later, Val carries on with what you were doing.

Hi Helen, report done I take it.

Yes, we now have a D.N.A. Read out for our boy, just need to match him up with someone.

That's the big question Helen.

How are you doing on the other
fronts, any further forward.

I wish I could say yes, but know it
is a slow process, but we will nail
it, I'm sure. Thanks for the report
I will pass some of it on to Clyde
Baker.
Their team in New York may spread
some light on this evidence, I'm
sure there is information they have
that will push this case on.

Good Luck.

Dan come into the office, these are
the photos taken of the body, see
this Tattoo, see if your computer
can work its magic see if you can
find anything about this group
online. Also, we have a partial
phone number, not sure if you can
work out the sequences of numbers we
need, to get a fix on the actual
number we are looking for. Is that
possible Dan.

Not sure, it would only give up the
number of random combinations,
Possible, so that could be quite a
few. So, if we find someone that
fits into that grouping of numbers,

117

there's a good chance that they know
who he is, name Etc.

I will leave that with you Dan,
here's hoping.

If anyone wants me, I've gone to the
Yard, to see Tony Knight.

OK Gov.

CHAPTER 13

Taking a trip out to the Yard, will
be going to memory lane, five years
since I was stationed there in the
Murder squad.
I would imagine the task force has
grown now, from my day. But I was
right to get transferred when the
opportunity came up, too many bosses
wanting to take the glory trail.
Tony's office still up on the fifth
floor, nice views over London
Yes, the office seemed to be crammed
ever more, with desks and computers.
How are you doing Vince a few of the
lads that new knew me shouted out,
come for your old job back Vince,
others commented.

No. Just thought I would check up on
you all, make sure none of you were

slacking.

We have more to do now, since you
have Bob over with your lot

Big Brian shouted, how are you doing,
out in the sticks Vince.

I'm enjoying it over there, but I'm
never too far from you lot, Family
alright Brian.

Yes, keeping good the eldest now
left college, she is into Fashion
designs.

Come in Vince, I hear your making
good progress with the case,

Yes, that's why I'm over here today.
Has Bob been keeping you informed.

He has been, on occasions, looks
like the Yanks want to step in now,
he tells me.

I believe this is fairly and
squarely in their court now.
Everything points to it starting in
New York but for why. it's an
unknown story now.
I've brought some of the photos, we
got from the path lab. This photo of
a Tattoo, we enhanced it bit, one of

119

the lads is trying to trace in on the Internet. that may yield some vital info for us. Then we have a partial phone number, again we had to get it enhanced to read it. I believe it is a U.K. number going by the prefix 07.

I would agree with that Vince, I take it you're doing a number check.

We are. I have spoken to the American Embassy people about these things, they were given copies to send to their counter parts in Brooklyn. They have since informed me that a Detective is coming over this week to add a bit more fire power to the case. I take you have been informed also.

Yes, they are bringing some files over, to share with us. So yes, looking good Vince.

Do you fancy a pint and a bite before I head off?

Now that's the best news yet, I take it the treats on you. This lot can manage without me for an hour.

Next morning the team were gathered in sorting out the bits and pieces

120

of information, but still no strong
lead to go with.

Dan how did you get on with that
Tattoo.

It seems they are a bad arse crowd
of fanatics regarding Second World
War collaborators, going by the
reviews I'm reading.
That Tattoo seems significant, if
you're a member you must have one.

Excuse me Gov, There's a Matthew
Kaufman at the front desk. Asking to
speak to someone on this case.

One of you go down and take a
statement from him.

I'll go Gov, Val Oats went out.

Good morning, Mr Kaufman, I'M
Detective Val Oats. What can I do
for you.

Some Detective's called in to see my
mother and Sister, regarding Rebecca
Finklestein, they said you wished to
speak to me also. I have been away,
So I thought I would just come in to
see you.

Would you like to follow me, need to

find an interview room, ah yes this
will be fine? Have a seat Mr Kaufman,
I will be back shortly, just need to
pick up some paperwork, would you
like a tea or coffee.

No, I'm fine thank you.
Here we are, we just want to recap
on your original statement from that
time, Is that OK for you.

Yes.

Great, your mother, and Sister were
very helpful with our enquiries.
Firstly, can you remember back to
that day in question what you were
doing when you first got up.

Well, I was awake for a while, on my
mobile trying to arrange a meet up
with my friends going to college, I
heard the front door being closed
early on, I presumed it was Dad,
going off to the shop.
I don't generally rush to get out,
either my mother or Sister seem to
take ages to use the bathroom, me
just a few minutes. I thought I
heard my sister leave, My Mums
bedroom door was still closed, that
usually meant she was not up. So, I
got in, used the bathroom, then left
for college/

Was there any sign of Rebecca, when you were still in the house?

Not that I recall, she was a free spirit, no rush to go anywhere except to the shops, she liked to compare our stuff, to what was back home. She liked going to the library. She also went up town on at least one occasion, to take in the sights Big Ben Trafalgar square Etc.

Had she made friends with anyone you know of.

Hard to say, unless she met someone at the library, the only place you could have a one to one with someone. I believe she spoke about a boy once, cannot recall his name, Chloe may well know.

Yes, she already told us, His name was Roy. He has been cleared from our original enquiries at the time. Is there anything you can remember from back then, since you've had time to think over the years?

No, it has cropped up now and again, I would wonder what happened to her. Sorry I cannot be of more help.

How did she socialize within the
family, any tension with the others?
Did she sit down and watch TV? with
the rest of you, that sort of thing.
No, we all have TV. In our rooms
generally, we don't sit down as a
family until dinner time.

The door opened with Addis,

Can I see you for a moment Val.?

Excuse me.

Yes Dan.

The Gov asked me to give you this,
ask Matthew if has seen it before,
or knows anything about it.

Is this the one from the body.

Yep.

Sorry about that, my colleague gave
me this to show you, as she pushed
it over to him to look at.

Do you recognise that, have you seen
it before?

Oh Yes, My Dad has one of those on
his Ankle.

On his ankle, how long has it been
there.

Forever, it is a cymbal from the
Wars, supporting the group from the
Holocaust, Holocaust. Victims.
Remembered. That's their initials
H.V.R. With the star of David.

Do you know when he had it done.

He told us when he was young, when
the War was just ending.

That's understandable at those times.
I think we have covered everything
Mr Kaufman. You have been very
helpful for us today we may need to
talk to you again, Another time.

That's no problem, Detective.

I will see you out,

Val could not wait to tell Vincent
the good news, we have a sort of
lead on the Tattoo.

Hi Val, as Vincent looked up from
his paperwork.

How did it go with the young Mr
Kaufman, could he add anything to

what we already know?

Oh yes Vincent, you're not going to
believe this, His father has that
Tattoo on his ankle.

At last, what did he say about it.

His Father has had it, since the War
Days, but his interpretation of the
initials is, Holocaust Victims,
Remembered. Do you think it's a
coincidence or a cover for the real
meaning?

Bring Addis in Val, let's have a
look at what we have.
Dan, check out the site again, see
if there is a parallel site for
these initials, they may be using it
as a cover, if there on this Dark
Web thing.
Val, put together everything we have
on him. I want to know what he had
for breakfast, need to dig deeper on
Mr Kaufman, you two get on with that,
The Detective from New York, is here
to see us he may be able to shed
some light on this.

Come through to the Vincent office
Brad.

Gov, this is Detective Brad Fillmore

from New York.

Hi, I'm Vincent Lusty, are we glad
to see you. Would you like a coffee
or a tea?

Yes, sweet and milky Vince.

Val, can you get a sweet and milky
tea for our guest.

Vince you will have to fill me in on
what you have and how you got into
this, I understand you have got some
photo's Etc, on the body that you
gleaned these bits of info.

Well, we have just discovered
someone living here, has that Tattoo,
from those War days. As you can see
it is very faint photo but that is
the best, we can get it due to the
state of the body.

Where a bouts on the body was it.

Ankle, Same as is the person living
here.

That's a good start, if they have it
there, it means they are a member of
this group. No doubting that, we
have seen quite a few.

127

I understand this was taken from the
body of your John Doe.

He was virtually a skeleton; we were
lucky to have found this much due to
the time he was in the ground.

Is this all you have, yes, I'm
afraid it is, we have a partial
phone number, but with numbers
missing, one of the computer geeks
is working on that, it's a U.K.
number going by the Area code.
If we can find the owner of the
number, we may well get our man.

CHAPTER 14

I have this file of stuff you are
welcome to look over, it will give
an insight to how this group works
and how the go about things. I'll
warn you, they can be very
imaginative, how they carry out
their Revenge on people, Innocent
people, just getting on with life,
but for a very small link to some
distant relative during the War. I
will leave this with you, so you can
digest what they are about. I have
an appointment at the American
Embassy with Clyde Baker. I will

come in tomorrow if that's alright
Vince.

Certainly, someone will be here I'm
sure, feel free to come and go as
you want too. Any help is most
appreciated.

You were right Gov they do have an
Internet presence, which looks quite
genuine. I would imagine people from
those times use it to keep in touch
with fellow suffers from the past.
It also shows, Abraham knows about
the DARK WEB, otherwise he would
have just come up with the normal
public site. He maybe savvier, than
we gave him credit for.

That's good, all we must do, is see
who is connected to which site. His
big Innocent excuses, that he knows
nothing card, might just catch him
out.

Good morning, Vincent, how we are
doing.

Good, we are looking into Mr Kaufman
now, the squad are finding out
everything we can about him. Before
we talk to him again.

That report you left me it is quite

substantial; the time alone must have taken years.

Yes, it did. The FBI. Were brought in some time ago, they have managed to put together quite a list of what they class as hate crimes. They suspect Murders are being committed, across the country.
There's no established pattern we can see. They use different methods for each victim it seems.

Yes, I noticed that no two are the same, but the one that crops up a few times, is traffic accidents, or Carjacking.
Also, no guns used, could that be a traceability factor, no loose ends.

Time does not seem to be a factor either.
The team set up a central information hub country wide, looking at all possible non-natural causes of Jewish deaths.
It is a small squad that is full time on this. They have been Trying to get someone on the inside for years. But it is very carefully orchestrated on their part. They go to great lengths to keep their work looking like normal everyday crimes. They don't advertise the fact it is

a contract killing. That's why they
have been so successful in their
mission, no matter how warped their
views may be.

Brad, You and I know, sometime,
somewhere, they will eventually make
a mistake.

Yes, each case, involves so many man
hours, to determine normal crime, or
a hit.

Excuse me Gov. Mr Kaufman travels to
the U.S. at least six to eight weeks
quite regular, stays sometimes a
week or just a couple of days, not
only New York, Chicago, Boston,
Vegas.

That's interesting Vince, we might
be able to connect the dots on some
hits against his flight data. When
we get a full list of data, I will
fax them over to New York.
Now what about your main suspect,
are we getting any closer to
charging him? he seems to have all
the connections to the girl, even
admitted as much.
Do you think him, and Kaufman are
together on this?

I was thinking that, whilst Abraham

has no Tattoo, Kaufman seems to be a member, according to you. Membership is this Tattoo; it cements their commitment. So, one has the other has not.

Could Kaufman have, Coerced Abraham to join this group. Then it all went wrong somewhere. Perhaps Abraham got cold feet, in the cold light of day, did he realise he was expected to do away with this girl.

There's that to it.

Excuse me Sir, Val interrupts, Abraham is downstairs to collect his computer stuff.

Val, take him into an interview room, we will be down shortly.
You can sit in on this Brad. See if he knows Kaufman, he might give something away.

Good morning, Mr Abraham, come to get your computer bits.

Yes, now you have done with them, I can get back to normal.

Whilst you're here, have a seat for a moment, I would like to ask a couple of questions if you don't

mind. This is Detective Fillmore
from New York he has joined our team
on this case.

What do you want to know now?

Do you know a Mr Kaufman?

NO. But I know of him, I was at
college with his son Matthew.

Did you meet his father?

Perhaps once, not sure. Has he
anything to do with this case.

You tell us Daniel.

How would I know, you just asked me
if I knew him?

So, you've had no dealings with him,
you don't really know him apart from
him being the father of one of your
classmates.

Is that all Mr Lusty, then I'm
leaving.

That was short and sweet Vince. What
about Kaufman, have you checked out
on his computers yet.

According to his children the house

computer was sold off and a much
faster up to date version is used,
it seems it is just for them and
their schooling. Mum and Dad do not
use it. They use their phones mostly.

Have you checked out his office
computers, not yet I think we will
take Addis with us, to see if we can
get his permission to look at his
hard drive on his computer? He said
he was very keen to help us, so we
will see if he's that helpful.

The Lewinsohn tailors' shop, is
situated quite close to Saville Row
The famous street of high fashion
tailoring for those who can afford
the luxury. The ground floor
elegantly decorated and furnished
with all the apparel required to
make their customers feel Special.

They were greeted by a tall well-
dressed gentleman in a dark well-
tailored suit, Company uniforms no
doubt.

Good afternoon gentlemen, how may I
help you.

We would like to see Mr Kaufman.

Do you Have an appointment Sir.

NO, can you tell Mr Kaufman Chief
Inspector Lusty, is here to see him.

Certainly, as he walked over to the
phone.

Mr Barber, can you show these
gentlemen, upstairs to Mr Kaufman's
office.

Giving the three of them a little
nod. Follow me please.

Mr Kaufman, these gentlemen have
come to speak with you.

Thank you, Barber. Do Come in, you
are not the Detective I spoke too
recently.
No, I'm Inspector Lusty, this is
Detectives, Fillmore, and Addis, I
believe you spoke with Detective
Russell before regarding Rebecca
Finklestein.

Such a sad thing is it still on
going. How may I help you today,
Inspector?

Well for eliminating purposes may we
check your computer system, also
your phone records, land line and
mobiles.

135

What will this involve, I cannot be
without our office computer for one
minute.

There will be no inconvenience we
hope. Detective Addis is going to
hook up to your system, with his box
of tricks to check things out for us.
If we can just commandeer your
computer for an hour. Is that OK,
meanwhile we can just have a chat
about your trips to the U.S.

That will be all right, anything to
help you get this sorted out
Inspector.

We see your travels, takes you all
over US. Is it business in all the
cities you visit?

Yes. I have a small company that
deals in the latest trends in
tailoring, it's a very cut-throat
business Inspector, you must keep
ahead of the competition.

How long have you been in this line
of business.

I would say many years, it's been a
family business started by my father,
I've been at it for a least fifty

years coming up.

Hi Mr Kaufman, I'm Detective
Fillmore from New York. Which areas
of the city are you trading in.

Rag trade area, suppliers, new
designer's innovations with new
exciting designs, the young are
drawn to couture work.
This filters down to the main
fashion lines, eventually.

So, you would have a large contact
base, of customers, and clients.
Are any of them aware of this case.

Not many, but some close friends,
were aware at the time.

Did you not inquire from these
people, your friends, or customer
base, about Rebecca Finklestein if
they knew her, or her name?

Not really, no one said they knew
her, did not recognise her name
either.

Did you not think, this was strange,
someone you say you met in New York,
you gave her your card, yet no one
can verify her, or her name? did
that not ring alarm bells under the

circumstances at the time.

Yes, I did think it strange, but the police were involved, I thought if I could not find her, they would. The police had checked her name or whereabouts but came to nothing, as well. As you know Detective, her passport was not genuine.

How many mobiles do you have, personal, business?

Six business, staff, myself, plus desktop in my outer office I have a laptop.

Ok Addis, start with the desktop, if that's ok with Mr Kaufman,

Certainly.

CHAPTER 15

Miss Dixon was sorting out appointments on the desktop.

Excuse me, I will need to take control of your computer for a little while, miss.

Oh, can I just finish this item, a couple of minutes.

Yes, that's fine, can I have a look
at your company mobile, while you're
doing that.
That's it there. OK.

Addis gets on with the downloading
all the information from the phone.

That's me finished with the computer
detective.

Great, we can swop seats then.

You must be very clever with
computers, to do all that stuff.
why do you need to do all that then?

Just police business, cannot really
say more than that.

Will you have to do all the
computers, and mobiles of the
company then. Sounds serious to me.

Yes, it is, a serious matter Miss.

I'm Anita Dixon

Addis had the desktop plugged in to
down the hard drive, Anita watched
has he set about taking notes on
what he was doing.

139

Can I tell you something, But I
don't want to get into trouble?

Tell me what exactly, what sort of
trouble.

Addis looked up to see Anita biting
her bottom lip and looking a bit
worried. But she had started now, no
going back

He won't sack me, will he?

Who Anita.

Mr Kaufman.

Why would he sack you?

I know he has other phones locked
away; I hear it sometimes when he is
not here.

How do you mean hear it?

Well along time ago I was just
finishing up for the day, I could
hear a faint ringing sound from Mr
Lewinsohn office, I thought he had
left his mobile on his desk, but I
could not see it anywhere. But I
traced it to the cabinet in the
office, which has a draw inside, He
always keeps it locked.

140

Did you tell him about it?

Yes, he told me not to worry, he keeps all his old phones, it must have been one of those that went off, he said.

I don't, think he will sack you for that Anita.

OH, that's all right then.

Ok Gov, that's the desktop done, also Anita's phone, may I have your laptop Mr Kaufman, it won't take long.

Is this necessary Inspector.

I'm afraid it is, also your mobile phone, also business mobile, as well. The quicker we get this done the better for everyone.

Addis was in his element, getting all this info he can check back at the office.

One more thing before we go Gov, the secretary, Anita informed me, that Mr Kaufman keeps all his old phones in a locked draw in that cabinet.

Mr Kaufman. The inspector challenged.

Now this really is not on, she had no right telling you about these mobiles, their very private.

Have you something to hide then, I thought you wanted to help get this matter cleared up.

I do, but these mobiles have nothing to do with your enquiries. They are very private.

We will decide that Mr Kaufman, if you please can you hand them over.

Have you a search warrant Inspector.

No but I can soon get one. If they are that private, we will use our own discretion in the matter, subsequently they will be returned to you. I would like to ask you one question about them, that is troubling me at this moment. These phones are cheap disposable phones. Why have you kept them, also why would you buy them in the first place, being you have access on your own mobile. That tells me you have something to hide Mr Kaufman.
Ok Addis can you bag them up
Thank you, Mr Kaufman we may be back, if there are any further details you

142

could help us with.

Back in the squad room, things were
not progressing in finding the
underlying cause of this case.
Vincent Lusty told his squad, right
listen up we need to start from
nothing again. Review what we have,
double check everything.
Addis, I would like you to chase up
on the Finnegans in Ireland. Have a
word with them, see what they know
on how the house was when thy moved
in.
Jim, I want you to find the Youngs,
see where their living now. You
better start from the last known
address
Carol, I want you to find out
everything you can on Mr Kaufman,
banking clubs etc, his business side
of things
Val, investigate the Abraham's, see
what they are up too. I would
concentrate on Danial the son first.
to see if any of them can be
connected to this H.V.R. group.

Excuse me sir, there's a gentleman
downstairs asking for you. A
professor Roberts.

For Christ's sake, ok tell him I
will be down shortly.

143

Hello Professor. I'm Detective inspector Lusty, what can I do for you. Ah you're the gentleman that brought the book in Grimms fairy tales is that right.

Yes, I did, I was wondering if it was a figment of my imagination or not.

Well, I cannot discuss what's going on, but I can tell you. You told Detective Russell; you had a gut feeling. Your gut feeling was right, that's all I can tell you for the moment.
I will get back to you, in the future, to let you know how it turned out. I would like you to keep this between us for the moment.

Yes, certainly Detective Lusty, sorry to have taken up your time. Good day, as he lifted his fedora. Back in the squad room everyone was beavering away, to try and find some sort of clue, to enable to get this case solved.
Addis, can you check the site initials on the internet again of this H.V.R. just to be sure.
Jim Russell made his way over to the forward address, given to them by

144

Daniel Abrahams for the young couple,
that lived in the house last.
Good morning I'm Detective Russell,
I'm trying to trace a young couple,
Mr Mrs Young.

That would be our daughter April,
and her husband Tony.

Do they still live here, this was
the last known address we have for
them?

No, they live out at Hendon, have
done for some years.

Can you give us some contact details,
address, phone numbers etc. They are
not in any trouble; we are making
inquiries about the house they lived
in Union Street, Finchley.

Ah yes nice little place, they moved
here when there was talk of the
council re-developing the area.

I'll get their details for you.
Here we go that's their new address,
first phone number is April's, tony
the second one.

Thanks for your help. one more thing
did you have any keys to their house.

Yes, at the time, we gave them back
to April, when they were moving out.

Addis did you get hold of the
Finnegans yet.

Yes sir, they lived at the house
just under ten years, it was them
that put in the vegetable bed in the
garden, also left the small shed
there. Nothing un-toward happened
whilst they stayed there. They gave
their notice in. Then retired back
to Ireland as planned. They returned
the house keys back to the agent's
office.
Val, how you are doing with Abrahams.

Well, when Mr Yudin senior died, the
business was passed down to the
current Mr Yudin. Who in turn hired
Abrahams to look after the business,
as you know he runs his own meat
company. Also, that Abraham got his
son involved with the business, as
he was near retirement, too much for
him to do all the work, on his own.
The company makes a profit, nothing
big though. A large portfolio of
property is where the money lies.
The son on the other hand has had a
checker career, dropped out of uni,

done a few menial jobs, until his father roped him in, doing the repairs etc on the properties.

Keep at it, Val.

Hello Jim, any luck with you.

Yes, got the details of the young couple, just going to give them a ring.

Carol, anything good on Kaufman yet.

He certainly travels a lot around the States, but mostly New York seems to be his main hub. Two of those   disposable phones Addis looked at, were used for contacts in New York. Turned out to be Gay clubs.

Is our man hiding more than we thought, any reference to Gay clubs here?

Seems to be one in Manchester.

Now this could throw a different light on things, I wonder if this is the reason, he was uptight about those phones. Have we got him all wrong in this case or is there more to come out.

Well Gov, perhaps he is a closet gay, why would he abduct her, he seemed to care for her and help her.

But she may have learned about his little secret, blackmail?

Come on Gov, she was only here for less than two weeks.

But she met him in New York, perhaps his guard was down over there.

So, she came here to blackmail him. She had his card, that he gave her, she could have just called him, safer I would have thought.

CHAPTER 16

I'm not sure Val, there is just something I think he is hiding from us; I don't think he is innocent, but I don't know on the other hand if he is guilty of anything either.

Yes Jim, the young couple are coming to the station.

Let's hope they can give us a lead in the right direction, give me a

148

shout when they're here.

GOV, they've just arrived,
downstairs.

Ok Jim,

Good afternoon, Mr Mrs Young. I'm
detective Lusty, this is detective
Russell, we are hoping you can help
us regarding your tenancy at 117
street Road. You've done nothing
wrong, so don't worry. I will ask
you some questions about the house
if you can just give us some idea
how the house was before you moved
out, ok.

Yes, fine.

I'll start at the beginning if I may.

How did you get the tenancy of the
house.

We applied at Yudin properties; they
advertise in the local press.

You went to their office? then what.

We had the choice of two houses we
could view, they gave us keys to
each house, we had to leave £5
deposit for each key to view the

houses, but we only took the keys to one house, the other house was not in the right area for us.

So, you took the keys and looked at the house.

Yes, it was well kept, as such and in good order, just needed some decorating done it was ideal at the time. We were saving to buy our own house, there was nothing to do, so we could move straight in.

Then what happened.

Took the key back, paid the deposit, that was it.

Did you use the garden?

Yes, had some barbeques sort of thing, just relaxed in the summertime on the lawn.

Did you at any time use the vegetable patch that was there.

No, that was not our scene at the time. But we do now, being a bit older, we have some ground at home now for growing vegetables etc.

Was there anything you noticed that

seemed odd, or out of place.

No, it was just a steppingstone
until we had raised a deposit for
our own house to buy.

What happened when you were giving
notice to leave and vacate the
property.

Nothing really there was rumours
that the council were going to
redevelop the area, so it was no
surprise.

So, you returned the keys of the
property to the agents.

We did that, also the keys our
parents had, handed them in got our
deposit back from the agents after
they inspected the house for damages,
they keep good records on what goes
on in their properties.

Have you ever been back there since
you left.

No, not much point, we have a nice
house in Hendon.

Can you tell us what this has been
all about?

151

Not really, it's just gathering some
details, of an ongoing investigation
we are looking into. You have been
very helpful in giving us a picture
of the time you were there. My
Sargent will see you out, thanks
once again.

Jim, I think we should have another
word with the Abrahams, if he keeps
such god records, that may hold the
key.
I think we will call it a night, see
you in the morning, we can look at
all the information we have, then go
over to see the Abrahams.

Morning Gov, Addis shouted out from
behind his computer. What
about checking the mobiles Gov, we
know they were used to phone this
gay club, can we not check the club
to find who the calls were for,
someone there may be able to help us
out there.

Good thinking Addis, get on to it.
Jim you ready, let's go over to see
the Abrahams.

Yudin's meat wholesale was a hive of
activity, lorries getting hosed down
after their mornings work.

This way Gov, the Abrahams have an office round the back.

Good morning, we are here to see the Abraham's.

Have you an appointment gentleman.

No, I'm detective Lusty, and this is detective Russell.

Excuse me Mr Abraham, there are two detectives here, they wish to have a word with you, ok, second door on the right down the hallway.

Good morning, Mr Abraham, I'm detective Lusty, I don't believe we have met, you know detective Russell.

Yes, gentleman how can I help you.

As you know we are looking into the property in Union Street that you once owned.

Yes, I'm aware of that, I thought we covered everything last time.

Just a few more questions we need to get cleared up. Will Daniel, be here this morning.

No, he is doing a couple of repairs,

153

on one of our properties today.

Perhaps you might be able to clear
up some things for us.

I will try, as you know Daniel is
more hands on than me

Now we understand, that when you
have a proposed tenant who wants to
rent a property, you give them the
keys to view the property, to see if
it's suitable, is that correct.

Yes, we do, they leave a key deposit
of £5 for that. In the past people
just never returned the keys if they
were not interested.

Do you, or did you keep a record of
those people who viewed the
properties at all.

I believe Daniel did keep records of
that.

Do you still have those records, if
so, may we have a look at them?

I would gladly show them to you.
Trouble is Daniel keeps everything
like that on his computer. It saves
a lot of paperwork. And I do not
know how computers work, you need

154

passwords etc he tells me. I believe
he can print out things like that,
the list I mean.

That would be helpful for us. So
that's always been the system used.

Yes, I will get him to drop the list
into the station for you.

When the property was empty, some
two years I believe, due to the
council's intended redevelopment of
the area.

Yes, that's correct, a lot of wasted
time there, we lost money on that.

So, what happened then, the house
goes up for rent again.

No, we decided to sell that house,
you cannot trust the council, they
may try again for redevelopment of
the area, we got out whilst the
going was good.

Was it up for sale long.

It took longer due to the area going
into decline, people were not
investing in the area. A few people
from the synagogue showed some
interest, one even viewed the house

but in general they were out to make a killing with silly offers, so we put into the hands of an estate agents Jacobson's.

Thanks Mr Abraham you've been most helpful. Nothing else Jim, think we covered what we wanted to know.

Yes, oh just one thing more, the person that viewed the house, did you give him any keys by any chance.

He collected them on the following Monday, dropped them back in the afternoon, not suitable for his son or daughter he said.

Can you remember his name?

Jack Kaufman.

Lusty and Russell looked at each other, thanks again Mr Abraham.

CHAPTER 17

Now that's a result Jim we can now place Kaufman at the house, I think he is connected to this case in more ways than one. If Addis can get any more info from those phones, it might just break the case for us.

156

We need to get him in to answer some more questions.

But he could say, yes, he viewed the house, then what gov.

I think he had a copy made of those keys, empty property to use. Phone Abraham back asking how long the house was sitting empty before he gave it to Jacobson's. I'll be in my office.

Hi gov, about five to six weeks the house was empty.

Ok, contact Kaufman, ask him to come into the station in the morning.

Addis how are you getting on with those phones.

Getting their sir, might have a lead soon, they are getting back to me.

Excuse me Sir a Mr Kaufman is downstairs.

Come on Jim, let's see what he has to say.

Thanks for coming in Mr Kaufman, I see you brought a solicitor with you.

157

I have, this is Mr Woolf.

Take a seat gentleman.
Firstly, can I ask you about 117
Union Street Finchley.

In what regards.

Do you know the property at all.

No, never heard of it.

So, you have no idea where Union
Street is. You've never been in the
house then.

Not to my knowledge.

Well, you have no idea where it is,
you've never been inside the house
then, if you don't know the address.

That's correct.

This leaves us with a quandary, Mr
Kaufman. You see Mr Abraham, of
Yudin properties informs us you do
know the address, also you have been
in the house, when you viewed it, to
see if it was suitable for your son
or daughter.

Ah yes, I viewed a house that he was
about to sell, I thought it might

158

have been suitable for one of my
children. Sorry I did not realise it
was that house it was a spur of the
moment thing, get the house cheap
perhaps.

Did you have copies of keys Mr
Abraham gave you.

What would be the purpose of doing
that. I had no interest in the house
as I told Mr Abraham.

Is this relevant to my client
inspector, surely viewing a house is
not a crime.

It is when a murder took place there.

Did you notice anything untoward
when you viewed it.

Some bits of old furniture, most of
the house looked like it had been
cleared out, due to the council
redevelopment.

You seemed well informed on the
matter, being you denied knowing the
house.

And you say you never had keys
copied.

No, what are you insinuating here?

I believe you had a spare set of keys cut, for what purpose I'm not sure yet. Perhaps a meeting place for your Gay liaisons.

Now listen here inspector, I'm not gay, I have no liaisons with anybody.

Inspector can you explain this line of inquiry.

Yes of course, your client was in procession, of some cheap phones hidden in his office, they have been used to phone a Gay club in Manchester, called HIM & HER. We are investigating this now, perhaps your client can explain this to us.

I believe at this stage I would like to have a conversation with my client alone Inspector.

That can be arranged. How long do you require?

I would suggest, we return tomorrow morning, that will give me time to assess my client's case, and how to advise him on what to say. I was under the impression when we came here it was for a simple interview.

Which is not the case. It seems it is more serious than what my client led me to believe. Would 10.30am tomorrow be acceptable Inspector.

That will be fine for us, I would like you to explain to your client, to tell the truth next time. He has been caught out today telling lies. Good day gentleman.

Well, that's a turn up for the books, Gov.

All we got to do is, get him convicted, I feel it in my bones, he is up to his neck.

Excuse me Gov, we have something from the club, apparently there was a regular at the club a Peter Katz. The caller always just spoke to him. Trouble is he's not been seen for quite some time. Has not been in the club for long enough. They gave us his mobile number; it is a fit with the partial number we have from the body recovered.

Great work Addis now we are getting somewhere. We can now ask Mr Kaufman. why he was phoning Mr Katz all the time. Well done everybody it's been

a good day; long may it continue.
Anyone up for a pint.

Count me in Gov, it seemed that
everyone was up for a little drink
or two, even the ladies.

Everyone in the office bright and
early, hoping to get all sorted out
now. Mr Kaufman. and his solicitor
arrived spot on time, led into the
interview room to carry on with the
questions.

Take a seat gentleman, so we will
pick up from yesterday.
Right, you were ringing the HIM &
HER club in Manchester, you always
spoke with a person called Peter
Katz. Can you explain why you were
always in contact with him.

Yes, he used to work for me, here in
London, he was learning the trade,
when he finished his time with me,
he moved north to Manchester. YES,
HE WAS Gay. but I'm not inspector.

So, you don't know why he died here
in London, or should I say murdered
here in London.

What do you mean inspector murdered?

That is exactly what I mean,
furthermore he was found at the
house you went too view, but you
said you never knew the house. Now
it transpires not only did you know
the house, but you also knew the
victim. Can you see why we are
interested in you Mr Kaufman.

But I never killed him or anyone,
for that matter.

I suggest you had a lover's quarrel
argued then you killed him.

.That is ridiculous,

Did you argue and quarrel, it got
out of hand.

No Comment.

You might as well tell us; we will
find out in the end.

No Comment.

You must see it from where we are
sitting, you did not know the house,
now you do. You were in a
relationship with Mr Katz you argued,

163

you tried to cover it up. Just come
clean admit it. You will feel better
for it.

No Comment.

How did you manage to hide the body
did someone help you, a job for two
people at least, hiding a body, you
nearly got away with it to?

No Comment.

Do you admit, having spare keys cut
for the house?

No Comment

Inspector, my clients answered your
question to the best of his ability,
no point in carrying on with this
unless you can come up with some
more evidence that implicates my
client. I suggest we terminate the
interview.

Very well, but we will be re
interviewing him in the future, when
we have gathered some more
information. Which we will
undoubtedly uncover.

Thank you, Inspector, for your time.

Right lads have we any more info
come in that we can use.

Not now Gov, trying to find the next
of kin for Mr Katz, we believe he
had family up north that's why he
went up there from London.

Has Daniel Abraham left the list he
was supposed to give us yet.

Nothing yet in but I will check
downstairs Gov.

Val, Carol have you sorted out the
finances of the Abraham family, and
the Kaufman, any unusual dealings.

No, they all seem to be above board
Sir.
Mr Kaufman does use his credit card
quite a lot, with all the traveling
he does.

Need some more evidence, to put this
to bed.

CHAPTER 18

GOV. The Americans left a message,
can you go to their Embassy, as soon
as possible, alone, also bring the

Grimm's fairy tale book.
I told them you were interviewing a
suspect, when they called.

That sounds ominous, wonder why they
want to see the book, they have
already seen it.

Big, impressive building the Embassy,
let's see what's in store.

Yes, Sir how may I help you, the man
on the desk inquired.

I'm Detective inspector Lusty I've
an appointment with, Mr Baker They
asked me to come in and see them.

Lifting his notes up, ah yes LUSTY,
I will let them know you are here
Sir. Take a seat Detective Lusty.

Looking around the foyer, there was
a steady flow of people coming and
going, the lifts pinging quite
regularly. Then Clyde Baker appeared
from one of the lifts, beaming smile
on his face. Hello, Vincent, we meet
again, sorry to have kept you
waiting, but we are on the top floor.

No problem. As Vincent Lusty stood
up to shake his hand.

Right follow me Vincent, how are you
doing on your case.

Getting there, narrowed it down to
one person of interest, now, unless
you have something for us, to change
that.

Your see. Here we are after you,
Clyde Baker, hand out welcome to our
little world Vincent, have a seat.
The other men in the room never
stood up, just a friendly nod. No
introduction either but holding some
paperwork in his hand.

Firstly Vincent, what is discussed
in this room today does not go
beyond these walls, for security
reasons. Any such breach about this
meeting, would be denied it ever
took place.

This sounds rather serious Ted.

Yes, it is, very serious Vincent.

Have you heard of Mossad?

Yes, the Israel's secret service I
believe.

Well, it appears you have got into
one of their old cases from eleven

years ago. This Finkelstein case.

Christ, how did I manage that.

By starting your investigation, looking for Miss Finklestein. That's where this gentleman comes into it, I will not introduce him to you, again security reasons. But he would like to ask you some questions, if that's ok.

Yes, anything to help.

Hello Vincent, can you tell me how and why, you started this investigation, into Miss Finkelstein.

Yes, I can, it all started, with a local Professor in our town, he had bought a job lot of things from an Auction house. Amongst them was this book, in my briefcase.

May I look at it.

Here you go, it has a marked passage, as you can see.

Your case, stemmed from this message in a ten-year-old book.

The Professor thought it was genuine.
But it was also an old unsolved cold
case in our files, that's why we
continued with it.

That amazes me.

From our side of the fence Vincent.
We sent two young agents in their
twenties to New York to try and
infiltrate the H.V.R. A male, and
female, we chose a very young
looking female for her age. We
thought the younger members were our
best chance, of getting accepted
into the group. We changed her name
and appearance, gave her a false
passport, as you know. Unfortunately,
we believe she was found out,
somehow. But by then she had made
the acquaintance of Mr Kaufman. when
he was over for a visit to New York.
He gave her his business card. A
short time later she flew to the U.K
for safety, from this group Who at
the time were dishing out
punishments to current living Jews.
Of family members who were thought
to be collaborators during the
second world war. Their ideology was
to eliminate any female family
members that were living, to stop
the family line, like the victims in
concentration camps, their family

169

lines terminated.
We have in place our own teams of
investigators, finding collaborators.
Unbeknown to Rebecca, she had flown
into one of the senior H. V.R.
member's nest.
Who intern was horrified, that she
came to him. He wanted her dealt
with as soon as possible.
He contacted his old employee Peter
Katz, also a member, but he was away
in Australia. He would not be back
for at least two days.
But when he returned, the plan was
put into action, Kaufman would
capture Rebecca on some pretence,
take her to the house then Katz
would come down the next day to do
the business, get rid of Rebecca.
Fortunately, it all went wrong at
the house.

We believe what Daniel Abraham said
happened, Happened. Rebecca
confirmed all this.
When Rebecca was staying at Abrahams
flat, she contacted us. A three-man
squad was sent to the house, to get
rid of Katz, and clean up. Rebecca
was collected back to our
headquarters. She gave a full report,
informed us the involvement of Mr
Kaufman.
To avoid a prison sentence, he

became our mole, helping us to
disband this heinous group.
As for the young Rebecca she is
34yrs old now happily married with
two children. May I keep this book
Vincent, I would like to give it to
Rebecca, as a keep's sake.
Now the balls in your court Vincent.
He obliviously contacted us, once
solicitors were involved.

That has been some story from an old,
scribbled book of Grimms fairy tales.
Yes, I think that would be quite
nice for her. Just need to justify
to my team now, also why this case
is now done.
Nice talking to you gentleman, my
lips are sealed.

Here's the Governor back lads.
How did it all go.

You know the Yanks. All I can say is
the case is now closed Top secret
stuff pack everything away. Look I'm
off to see Kaufman. See you lot in
the morning.

Good morning I'm here to see Mr
Kaufman, go straight in Detective.
I'm aware you have powerful friends,
Mr Kaufman. There will be no more
interviews, I will get your mobiles

171

back to you in a couple of days. But
I'm glad this has all been sorted
out now.

Same here Inspector, no hard
feelings, just doing your job.

Printed in Great Britain
by Amazon

85006673R00106